Propagation

Also by D.H. Jonathan:

The "Volunteer"

Life Models

The Girl Who Stopped Wearing Clothes

The Tattoo Collector

PROPAGATION

A Novel by

D.H. Jonathan

Naturale Publishing

2026

Cover design by Paramita Bhattacharjee
(www.creativeparamita.com)

Visit the author's website at www.dhjonathan.com

First Edition

ISBN: 978-1-7330908-3-4

For my sons Seth and Elijah.

1

Pain and blinding light are the first things I experience as I open my eyes. I squeeze them shut again, throwing my arm over my face. All my joints hurt, muscles too. Everything hurts. There is a stinging in my penis and a dull ache below that. But it's the throbbing pain in my head that overshadows all the rest. I try opening my eyes again under the shadow of my arm. The white ceiling makes the light seem brighter, but I squint under my arm and try to let my eyes adjust to the light. I'm cold, and I realize that I am naked, lying on plastic. Why am I naked? This was supposed to have been just a simple memory upload.

I roll to one side, and my skin stings as it pulls away from the plastic surface with a soft ripping sound, and then I roll the other way. My eyes adjust enough to allow me to see the tiny scab in the middle of a bruise near the crook of my elbow. I remember the nurse sticking my arm to start the IV. The burning sensation in my penis makes me think they might have had me on a catheter? Why would they do that? The memory upload was supposed to take only a few hours at most. Had something gone horribly wrong? That white ceiling has all sorts of robotic arms folded up and at rest. I don't remember seeing those when I lay down for this procedure. Had I been moved?

Ignoring the throbbing ache in my head, I sit up and swing my legs to the side so that my feet rest on the floor. A wave of nausea makes me want to vomit, but I choke it back. My stomach feels empty, so I doubt there's much to throw up anyway. I take a few slow deep breaths as I survey my surroundings. I look down at myself and see that everything is wrong, but the thing the takes center stage is my penis. Why do I have foreskin? Did they reverse my circumcision while I was under? Is that even possible? I want to pull that foreskin back to see if this is the real me, but part of me doesn't want to touch it. What if it is someone else's?

This place doesn't look anything like Jordan's memory retrieval lab, at least not the parts of it I saw. There is a window high on the wall across from the space in which I sit. I'm not in a room, just in a little alcove in a long corridor. Outside the window across from me is blackness. Is it night? I want to get up and look out, try to figure out where I am, but my legs feel weak. And they look impossibly thin and hairy. Are they really my legs? How long have I been out that I've lost this much weight?

What the fuck is going on?

"Hello?" I call out, and my voice sounds too high pitched but also gravelly. My throat hurts.

Dead silence is all I hear. No one answers my call. Is there not any staff on duty?

"Anyone here?" I say in as loud a voice as I can muster, but the only answer is stillness.

I push up from the plastic pad on wobbly legs. I have to grab the wall beside the head of the bed to keep from face planting onto the floor. Once I've steadied myself, I let go of the wall and stand on my own without falling.

"So far so good," I say.

I take two steps away from the bed to where I can see up and down the corridor. It appears to be long, curving up in both directions.

"Oh my God," I say as I realize I'm on the *Armstrong*. "This can't be happening."

"Two months of intense training, then a memory upload, and then you go back to your regular life." That's what Jordan had told me during that first initial meeting. Is that what happened? Had I gone back home and lived out the rest of my days? If I'm on the *Armstrong* right now, then I'm not me. I'm a clone of myself, with those memories that had been uploaded, now downloaded into this brain. My brain. No. I can't believe it. I had, just a few hours ago, walked into the Memory Retrieval Center and lain down for the procedure. That had to have been today. I feel like I've just woken up from that. The upload was the last step of the two month training. I should be leaving now, heading to the San Francisco Airport to fly home to Rapid City. I guess the original me did fly home. Which means I'm not the original me. Jordan's mission plan, the one we all thought was crazy but went along with anyway because he was paying us a ridiculous amount of money, actually worked.

The window beckons. It is eye high, as if placed there for someone exactly my height. It is about seven paces across the corridor from me. My room, or pod as Jordan had called them during our training, is open on both ends, with no doors. It's just one stop on a big wheel. On the wall opposite my pod are a series of handles built into the wall at regular intervals. We had used them during training for moving through the wheel section when it was in zero gravity. One of those handles is directly below the window.

I shuffle over on unsteady legs. Grabbing the handle on the wall, I look out at a massive swirl of glowing blue and brown and white tumbling by, over and over itself. The motion brings the nausea roaring back. I gag and heave, but nothing comes up. Turning away from the window, I spot the lavatory next to the foot of the pod where I had awoken. I stumble that way until I can lean over the commode to continue my heaving, barely noticing the white powder on the floor. A little something green and yellow comes up and out of me. I cough and spit and flush it away. I want to wipe my mouth, but the roll for the toilet paper is empty. The paper towel dispenser next to the sink is also empty.

I stand at the sink meaning to rinse out my mouth when the image in the mirror stops me. Looking back is a young, emaciated face with long hair and sparse beard. Despite the unkemptness, that face can't be any older than eighteen. I'm forty-eight years old. Or at least, I *was* forty-eight years old.

"Holy shit. Jordan, you crazy son of a bitch." *Or I'm dreaming this. Please let me be dreaming this.*

I hadn't been able to get a look at the planet because of the nauseating spinning. My feet are firmly on the floor, so I know it's not the planet spinning. It's the wheel section of the *Armstrong*, rotating around the central command module to create artificial gravity. I wasn't able to discern the oceans or land masses below, and I'm not even going to try as long as the wheel is spinning. Is it Earth, or am I really out in deep space as Jordan had planned?

If this is real, if I really am a clone of myself out in deep space, where are the other five crew members? There's no sign of anyone else. If this isn't just a drug induced dream while knocked out and getting my memories recorded, why am I alone? Of course, if this is real, then, according to the mission plan that Jordan had laid out to us, the *Armstrong* has been orbiting the planet below for almost twenty years. It just stands to reason that we wouldn't all wake up at the exact same moment.

I turn on the sink and bend down to the faucet to rinse my mouth. Once done, I look at my reflection again. If I could shave and get a haircut, I would look exactly as I did at my high school graduation, minus about thirty pounds and plus one foreskin. This can't be real, I tell myself again. I still feel like me, even if my reflection doesn't look like it anymore. The mirror is the door of a small cabinet, so I open it and find a toothbrush and a razor still in the plastic packaging. There's also what looks to be an unused tube of toothpaste and a can of shaving cream. I rip the toothbrush out of the packaging and brush my teeth as thoroughly as I can. The shaving cream sputters and doesn't cover much when I try to rub it onto my chin, but I shave anyway. There is also a brush in the cabinet, so I run it through my long tangled hair until I get it somewhat straight.

There is a shower stall next to the commode, and if my legs weren't starting to feel so shaky, I would probably make use of it. As it is, I stagger back to my pod and sit on the edge of the bed. I'm still naked. I should probably get dressed before figuring out what to do next. There should be five sets of blue uniforms in a drawer under my bed. I kneel on the floor, feeling too tired to stand, and pull the drawer out. Inside is a cloud of faded blue fuzz like dust. I run my hand through it and watch some of it float up and fall back down into the drawer. There is nothing solid. The bottom drawer contains what used to be casual tennis shoes. The rubber soles are intact, but the cloth and shoestrings are just masses of fuzzy powder. OK, maybe I won't get dressed. But why would someone vaporize my clothes? Is this some kind of weird joke Jordan is playing? Like most billionaires, he is a bit eccentric, but this would be too elaborate even for him.

A high-pitched shriek from down the corridor pierces the silence and sends chills through my body.

"Hello?" I say, using the wall for support as I make my way on wobbly legs toward the sound of the wailing.

A childlike sob is the only answer I hear before the shrieks start again. The next pod along the corridor is just like mine, with a bed, a window, a chest of drawers, and a lavatory, except that a plastic canopy covers the bed. I pause ever so briefly to look through that canopy and see a tiny skeleton, either a fetus or an infant. I have to ignore what this means for now as I search for the source of those ear-splitting shrieks.

The next room is empty, not even a skeleton in the bed, although the plastic canopy still covers it. In the third room, a naked teenage girl lies on the floor between the bed and the window. Her black hair is long and wild and covers most of her face. Her long legs are splayed apart, unselfconsciously exposing her vulva. When she sees me, the shrieking stops, and she tries to scoot back into the corner, her expression, what I could see of it through the hair over her face, one of unmitigated terror.

"It's OK," I say in as calm and soothing a voice as I can muster. "I'm not going to hurt you."

The girl wails again as she tries to back further away as if hoping the wall could somehow absorb her. My legs finally give out, and I sink to my knees. The girl has curled into a ball, arms around her knees.

"Hey," I say, holding my hands out, palms up. "I don't know what's going on either."

She grunts, looking at me through that long mess of hair.

I see the name plate on the side of the bed below the mattress. *L. Bascombe*, it reads.

"Linda?"

I reach forward to move the hair from her face. The Linda Bascombe I knew was a 62-year-old anthropology professor. I had seen her just before walking into the Memory Retrieval Center, seemingly a few hours ago. Linda has gray hair usually worn up in a bun and seems shorter and a lot heavier than this feral looking teenager. Still, something in the shape and color of this girl's eyes tells me that she is, indeed, an eighteen-year-old clone of Linda. There is no recognition of me in those eyes, only fear.

"It's me, Kevin," I say.

I stroke her upper arm with a feather-like touch. She flinches, and I wait to touch her again.

"It's all right," I say. "Can you talk?"

She just looks at me. I touch her again, softly like a caress, on the shoulder. She doesn't flinch away this time.

"It's OK," I say in that gentle voice. "We'll figure this out."

I roll into a seated position next to her, maintaining that contact. I was thinking she might try to run away, but I quickly realize that she probably can't even walk.

"Give me a few minutes."

I sit, gently stoking her arm and shoulder, and try to figure out what the hell I should do now.

2

The mission, as Jordan Walker had explained it to me at that preliminary meeting in his San Francisco office, which was the first time I had seen him in over twenty years, was to ensure the propagation of the human species by expanding into the stars. This was just two years after he said in an interview published in *Vogue* that manned exploration outside of our solar system would never be feasible because of the limitations of physics. "We will never have the capability of building a space craft that will even approach, much less exceed, the speed of light," he had claimed.

Jordan was a billionaire, most of that fortune earned from the Ion Automobile Corporation, makers of hydrogen powered vehicles and the infrastructure to support them, which soon eclipsed the battery-powered electric cars that had dominated the market for a decade or two. He had also bought most of SpaceX after Tesla struggled to switch from electric to hydrogen and had expanded manned operations on the moon and Mars. So if anyone had a question about the feasibility of interstellar travel, Jordan would have been the preeminent person to ask.

"I had to expand my thinking," Jordan had replied after I mentioned the *Vogue* article.

And expanded it, he had. The trip would take thousands, if not tens of thousands of years, he told me. Incredible advances had been made in both human cloning and in memory recording and transference. I have little doubt that he had funded and driven most of those advances.

"The crews will consist of two men and four women," Jordan had said from behind his big desk, his fingers flicking a purple fidget spinner.

"Crews, plural?" I had asked.

Jordan gave me a sheepish smile. "Yes. Six crews, same six people on each one."

"The same six on each?"

Jordan shrugged, that sheepish smile never leaving his face. "Like I said, I had to expand my thinking."

All six ships were called the *Armstrong*. Each would have a pre-programmed destination in mind, six planets where the probability of conditions for human habitation was high based on what we could determine from such a distance.

"Everything on the planet has to be right: atmosphere, temperature ranges, geology, non-sentient life for food, protection against radiation from space. The conditions here on Earth are so delicate, and the chances that all of those conditions are comparable on any one of those six planets is low. But having six ships with six different destinations increases those odds."

The ships would leave with six frozen embryos with our DNA. The cold of space would keep the embryos frozen as they would be traveling with no power. When the ship got close enough to a star's energy, it would power up, and the on-board AI would take over. It would analyze the entire star system, concentrating on the target planet. If no planets capable of sustaining human life were found, the AI would calculate a slingshot maneuver, using the star's gravity to pick up speed, shooting the ship out into the unknown where it would hurtle through space until it came across another star. The process would then repeat, with the AI searching for a hospitable planet.

When such a planet was finally found, the AI would make the necessary course adjustments and put the ship in orbit around that planet. The embryos would then be activated and grown in automated pods, kept alive but in an induced coma until sometime around their eighteenth birthdays. The recorded memories would then be downloaded into the brains of the clones shortly before being awakened.

I want to go home. I miss Cynthia, my wife. I miss Thomas, Kaitlyn, and Bobby, my three kids. I miss my house in Box Elder, South Dakota. And I'm never going to see any of them again. The realization hits me like a bulldozer. In some other reality, I woke up from the memory upload procedure, left San Francisco, flew to Denver and then to Rapid City where I was met by Cynthia and the kids, at least Kaitlyn and Bobby as Thomas was back in Texas starting college, and driven home after a long two months of astronaut training. But that's not my reality. Therefore, that's not me. Even though I have his memories, I am not Kevin Stiles. I'm something else. Someone else.

The *Armstrong* has been in orbit here for almost twenty years. I have to tell myself this because it still feels like I was in the Memory Retrieval Center just a few hours ago. But since the ship has been in orbit so long, I'm not worried about the *Armstrong* itself. The ship seems to have done just fine on its own. I do need to account for all five of my fellow crew members. I know one of them didn't make it, and probably two. I didn't look at the name plates on those two pods I passed as I was concerned with the wailing.

This girl, who is not Linda Bascombe but looks like she could be a much younger and skinnier version of her, soon tires of sucking her thumb and begins crying again.

"Linda," I say.

Her crying just intensifies at the sharpness of my voice.

"I'm sorry," I say in my soft, soothing tone.

Whatever memory download that worked on me didn't quite happen with her. She acts like an infant. Jordan and I had talked about the possibility of this happening, with Jordan assuring me that the chances were slim. I plan on telling him that slim had just shown up. If his clone survived the trip, that is.

Linda is crying like my kids did when they were

hungry. Come to think of it, I'm hungry too. I caress her upper arm again.

"I'm going to go try to find us some food," I say, although I don't know why. She doesn't understand a thing I'm saying. "I'll be right back."

I struggle to my feet, my skinny legs wobbly, but then again, I have never used them before today. It's a strange thought, but it's true. This body has been lying in that pod ever since the embryo was activated, or whatever it is that Jordan called it. I feel my belly and find the navel there, just to make sure I have one. I would have been fed via something like an umbilical cord from something like a placenta for the first forty weeks or so after the embryo activation. Those had been part of what had been frozen. After those first forty weeks, a conventional feeding tube and an IV would have been used.

Using the wall for support, I make my way along the corridor, passing another room with a pod. The plastic canopy is still closed on this one too. I look inside and see the mummified body of another child. This one looks to have survived longer, at least five or six years. The name plate below the bed of the pod reads "L. Markum".

"Sorry Lilly," I say. I don't know whether to feel sad or not. The real Lilly Markum lived out her life on Earth and is being spared whatever this is that Linda and I are going through. I guess I'm sad that I won't get to see her and talk with her.

Other than Linda's crying, the ship is still silent. We may be the only ones left. That thought scares me, especially since Linda isn't really Linda. There should only be one other pod to check. I'm pretty sure that the closed empty pod was a failure. If someone had awoken and moved to another part of the ship, I would think that the pod would still be open like mine and Linda's are. I need to go back and look at the name plates on those other two pods, but I keep going forward to check the last one.

I don't have to bend down to look at the name plate in the last room. The decaying male body encased in its glass pod tells me everything I need to know. This was Jordan's clone. He was the only other male on the ship. Linda and I are the only ones alive. And out of six, I am the only one that was regenerated with full memories as planned. A thought occurs to me that perhaps not everything worked with me and that as time marches forward, I will discover things wrong with me. There's nothing I can do about it if it happens, so I discard the thought.

Jordan's facial features are almost recognizable even though the pale gray skin seems to barely cover the skull and bones. It appears that the clone body had lived until its early teen years. I can't help but wonder what had happened.

"What the hell do I do now?" I ask the body.

I can almost hear Jordan's voice saying *Carry on with the mission.* With a sigh, I turn and continue on to the storage room. I remember that it is just past the last pod. The first cabinet I open is filled with dozens of vacuum wrapped cases of paper towels, toilet paper, and cleaning soap. Each vacuum wrapped package is attached to its shelf via Velcro. I am reminded of the empty toilet paper roll in my lavatory and of the white powder all over the floor. Had the toilet paper somehow disintegrated? And had the clothing in my drawer done the same thing? I wonder what will happen to this toilet paper if I open the vacuum packs, but I don't have time to conduct that experiment now. I close that cabinet and move to the next one. Cans of protein powder fill the top two shelves, also vacuum packed in clear plastic packages with six cans in each. I pull one of the packages down and struggle with the tab that is supposed to open the seal. In the other room, Linda's crying seems to take on a new urgency. I finally get the pack ripped open, and all six cans fall to the floor and roll in different directions. I grab one, feeling dizzy after bending over and straightening back up. I find two plastic cups on another shelf and take all of this back toward Linda's room, ignoring the corpse in the pod on the way. When I get near Linda's wailing, I stick close to the wall so she doesn't see me and get more upset than she already is. I then slip into the lavatory.

I fill the cups up to three quarters full from the faucet, and then put two scoops of the powder into each. I'm guessing as to the water to powder ratio, but I'm in a hurry because Linda's crying is so grating on my nerves and my eardrums. The cups don't have lids, and I don't have any spoons. To mix the powder and the water, I pour as much as will fit into one cup and then pour it back into the other cup. After about four times doing this, I have what looks like two normal protein shakes. I take a sip of one and grimace as it tastes like flavored chalk, but my stomach growls in response. I down it in three big gulps and rinse the cup, using that cup to first rinse the taste out of my mouth and then to take a long drink of water.

I carry the other cup into the room where Linda still sits crying on the floor. Her cries intensify when she sees me.

I sit cross-legged beside her, lowering carefully so I don't spill her protein shake. Some of it spills anyway as Linda grabs me by my shoulders as soon as my butt touches the floor.

"Easy," I say in what I hope is a soothing tone.

Linda continues to cry, and I bring the edge of the cup to her mouth. I tilt it just enough that a small amount of protein shake hits her mouth. Linda stops crying as she swallows and then runs her tongue over her lips.

"I'm sorry about the taste," I say to her even though I know she doesn't understand.

When I bring the cup to her lips again, she gulps it down as if it's the best tasting stuff in the universe. It occurs to me that Linda—this Linda anyway—has no memory of taste. My protein shake did taste a bit like baby formula which seems to make it appropriate for her. Linda coughs after swallowing too much at once, with protein shake covering her chin. Some of it splatters on my chest from her cough. I can't help but laugh. Linda looks at me, her head tilted like she wants to ask a question, and then smiles at me. She doesn't laugh but does look at the cup in my hand. I hold my finger under her bottom lip to catch any spillage as I tilt the cup to her mouth. She gulps it down, less of it spilling from her mouth than before but enough to soak my hand. I try to pull the cup back, but she grabs it and tilts the back of it upward, spilling more of the protein. When the cup is empty, Linda takes my hand and puts my fingers in her mouth, sucking as much of the protein mixture as she can get. This amuses me until she bites down on my index finger.

"Ow!" I yell and pull my hand away from her.

"Ugh," she says and smiles again.

"Your teeth hurt," I tell her.

Linda takes the cup from me and licks the inside of it as far as her tongue will allow. I stand up to go back to the supply room to find something to use to clean ourselves. Linda drops the cup and lunches forward to try to grab my lower leg. I dance back, almost falling down. I'm still not used to how weak my body feels.

"I'll be right back," I tell her for the second time in the past few minutes, my hand stroking her head.

She looks at me with pleading eyes, and I almost stay. But I also know that I have things to check on, so I walk away despite her cry of anguish.

3

There's nothing much to see in the two pods I had passed when searching for Linda's wailing. The empty pod has the name S. Patterson on it. Stacey had been a statuesque blonde. I peer through the clear plastic, trying to see any sign of a body. If Stacey's clone had died in the embryonic stage, there wouldn't be anything visible. I continue on to the next pod, the one just before mine. Now that I'm really looking, I see that there isn't much left of the remains. She'd died early on, before most of the bones had solidified. This would have been Kacey, a freckled redhead who had been an airline pilot in her original life. This meant that it would be up to me to get us down to the planet surface whenever that time came, if, for some reason, the Artificial Intelligence failed or faltered. Great. Nothing like the weight of the entire human species on your shoulders. I guess I'm lucky that that weight isn't much, the human species only consisting of two living members.

Just for fun, I open the drawer under Kacey's pod and find the same pile of blue fuzz and dust I had found in mine.

"Who needs clothes anyway?"

I walk back into my own pod and sit on the side of my bed, thinking about the crew we were supposed to have had here.

I had to walk through a gauntlet of reporters to get into the building. Luckily for me, none of them knew who I was. They were all looking for Jordan Walker, the eccentric genius who was sinking two billion dollars into a mission to the stars to help ensure the continued survival of the human race. Two billion dollars, and no one alive would ever know whether the mission was successful or not.

It was the first day of a two-month training program designed to ingrain in us all the mental, emotional, and intellectual experience we would need when our clones were activated. Physical training didn't matter, Jordan had told me, as our bodies would be entirely new to us upon waking. The physical training would be conducted with us in our clone bodies as we prepared to leave the *Armstrong* in orbit and travel to the surface of whatever planet the AI had found for us.

I was escorted into an ornately decorated conference

room, an oil painting landscape of a valley in Yosemite National Park on one wall and a large floor-to-ceiling window overlooking the San Francisco Bay on another. I sat across from a vaguely familiar woman who looked to be in her sixties. She wore a frilly blouse with a tweed jacket and had her long gray hair tied in a ponytail. I wore a polo shirt and blue jeans and wondered if I shouldn't have dressed in something nicer.

"Good morning," I said.

She nodded to me. "Hello."

Before I could introduce myself, three attractive young women were ushered into the room. They laughed and seemed to already know each other. The laughter stopped when they saw the two of us already seated.

"Hello," a thirty-something blonde in a San Jose Sharks t-shirt and blue jeans said.

I stood and offered my hand. "Hi, I'm Kevin Stiles."

The blonde shook it. "Stacey Patterson."

The other two women, one African American and the other a redhead with bright auburn hair, looked like they were about to speak when Jordan swept into the room with two aides.

"Good morning, everyone," he said, heading to the head of the conference table. "I've got a full agenda today, so why don't you all sit down, and we'll get started."

The two aides arranged Jordan's notes on the table in front of him as he sat, positioning his laptop just above those notes. He nodded to them when all was as he wanted it, and they vacated the room. I waited for everyone else to get situated before taking my own seat. Before I could even begin to wonder about Jordan's motivations for choosing such beautiful women for our crew, he had picked up his fidget spinner and started into his remarks.

"I'd like to welcome all of you to the crew of the *SS Armstrong*, the SS standing for starship. This is a mission for all mankind, not just one country. Each of you was hand picked by myself based on a combination of factors, genetics, intelligence, education, medical history, and just plain intestinal fortitude. You all know me, of course. I only chose people I already had some connection to. But I thought we'd go around the room and have each person introduce themselves for everyone else. So, without further ado."

Jordan motioned toward the older woman across from me since she was sitting closest to him. She sat up straight and cleared her throat.

"My name is Linda Bascombe. I've been a professor of anthropology at the University of Arkansas for the past twenty-six years." She looked at the other three women. "Jordan was one of my students back in 2032 as was Mr. Stiles here." She motioned toward me.

I looked toward Jordan who just shrugged and tapped his temple as if to say that the woman was brilliant.

"I earned my PhD at Stanford University in 2028. Before that, I played small forward for the Dallas Wings of the WNBA."

Dr. Bascombe sat back as if done with her presentation.

"And what made you decide to join this mission?" Jordan asked.

She took a deep breath. "I have to confess that I was torn. Throughout human culture, every belief system except atheism has prescribed to the theory of an afterlife, that each person has a soul. If we are to do this, agree to be cloned and have our memories transferred to that clone, how does that affect our belief in this? And more importantly, how does it affect the perception of the clones who wake up with our memories? This is new technology. We've never been able to record and move the entire memories of a person before. Do those memories constitute our 'souls'? Will those clones with our memories essentially become us, or will they be their own individuals, capable of making decisions that we ourselves would never make? These questions shouldn't be discarded as, Jordan, you seem to be doing."

Jordan started to answer, but Dr. Bascombe held up a hand to stop him.

"On the other hand," she continued, "the chance to not just observe but to be a part of the creation of a whole new human culture was too great to resist even if no one currently alive will ever get to read my observations of such a thing."

The more Dr. Bascombe talked, the more I remembered sitting in her classes in Fayetteville listening to her lectures. She was much younger then, and I recalled that most of the guys, myself and Jordan included, were hopelessly infatuated with her.

"Thank you, Dr. Bascombe," Jordan said. "We are lucky to have you on this mission."

Linda, the original Linda, was a thinker and a philosopher. During the two month training, I had spent more time with Linda than with anyone else. At first, it had been just because she had been one of my undergraduate professors, but as training progressed, I grew to value our deep conversations on a variety of topics but mostly about what this mission meant. The loss of her intellect and her conversation hits me harder than the deaths of the other four crew member clones. I rise from my pod and begin to make my way back to Linda's, recalling a conversation we'd had in her room after the centrifuge had made her sick for a day.

"Are we learning how to survive in space or how to make ourselves sick?" she had asked.

"Both," I replied with a laugh.

"I hope younger me is better able to handle it than old me."

"You're not old."

"Yes, I am. Too old for astronaut training anyway." She paused and looked past me. "I wonder how that will feel, to have my mind, my memories, in such a young body. Will an eighteen-year-old brain be physically capable of storing sixty-two years of memories?"

"An even bigger question is, will the eighteen-year-old brain with sixty-two years of memories be able to record the memories of the next sixty-two years?" I had said.

Original Linda had nodded and said, "Hmmm."

Knowing that Linda will never be able to experience being in that young body, at least not in this iteration of the *Armstrong,* saddens me even further. *Have to concentrate on the here and now*, I tell myself.

"Oh shit," I say when I see clone Linda still on the floor next to her pod.

It hits me a second later that my exclamation was a very literal description of the problem before me. How do I potty train someone when there are no diapers in her size to be had?

4

I struggle as I carry Linda into the shower, trying to get her to support some of her own weight by letting her feet touch the floor. She never gets the message as I wind up almost dragging her. Linda cries until I get the warm water flowing on her. Since we are both already naked, it's easy to get her cleaned up. I find a bar of soap and a bottle of shampoo in the vanity under the sink and wash us all over. Parts of me are still sore from whatever medical things had been hooked to me, and I'm sure that's the case for Linda as well. She clings to me as we sit on the floor of the shower stall, the water streaming onto us, rinsing the soap and shit and dust from our bodies.

"We've got to get you walking," I say. "If I'm physically able to walk, you are too. You just have to grasp the concept."

Linda grunts in response. At least she recognizes that I am talking to her.

"I'm sorry," I tell her. "You were brilliant. I mean, you should be brilliant right now. I don't know what happened."

Linda just stares at me, blinking her eyes slowly. Once we are cleaned and rinsed, I turn the water off and continue to sit with her. After we have drip dried with only our back sides wet from sitting on the shower floor, I pick her up and try to carry her back to my room, having to stop to rest twice because I feel so weak. At least she doesn't weight much. When I set her on the bed, she immediately lies back and curls into a fetal position. I stand over her for a few moments, watching as she seems to fall asleep, before heading back toward the supply room to look for cleaning materials for the floor in her room.

Before I get there, I stop and look in the bathroom next to her pod. I find a bucket, a brush, and a bottle of bleach under the sink in her bathroom, and I clean the floor from my knees. The mess is minimal, and it doesn't take long to clean it up. Most of it had been left on her body and had gone down the shower drain.

When I finish cleaning, I'm exhausted, and I want to be lying on one of the plastic mattresses just as Linda is. But my curiosity about the *Armstrong* is too strong to squelch right now. I have to at least make a loop around the entire wheel. The other side of the floor beneath my feet is actually the outer wall of the ship. The spokes leading to the large cylinder section, what Jordan had called the service module, would therefore go up from what I perceive as the ceiling. I see a hatch that leads into one of those spokes above me here in the storage area. I could open that hatch and climb that ladder any time, but we'd have to stop the wheel's turning to actually get into the service module. Stopping the wheel would put everything into zero gravity. So I shouldn't ever have to climb that ladder, just use it to push myself to the service module. I remember Jordan telling me that after our clones were activated, we'd have to spend the equivalent of up to two years on the *Armstrong* and that if we spent it in zero g, our bodies wouldn't be able to handle the gravity down on the planet. So, as long as everything works fine, I won't be going to the service module any time soon.

I walk past the supply room and into what looks like a modern health club. Six treadmills, six stationary bicycles, and six resistance machines sit in a row. Other than some light dumbbells on a rack behind the stationary bikes, there are no weights. Full weight machines must have been too heavy for space travel into and out of Earth orbit. For all I know, they're too heavy for interstellar space travel too.

After stopping for a moment to catch my breath, I continue into what looks like a lounge area with two couches and a large view screen. The couches look to have been shredded at some point, the cloth upholstery a fuzzy mess like my clothes and shoes had been.

"What the hell?" I say to myself.

I don't know why cloth and paper seem to have disintegrated, but I'm not going to spend energy right now trying to figure it out. I move on to the next space which appears to be a control room of some kind. There is a large view screen on the far wall with a console in front of it, kind of like a miniature Mission Control in Houston. The chairs at these consoles are made from the same type of plastic as the mattress on which I woke up, so, unlike the couches, they are intact. I sit at one of the chairs and punch Enter on the keyboard. The small monitor on the console and the big view screen on the wall come to life, both displaying a somewhat stationary image of the planet below. I don't recognize any of the land masses visible through the cloud cover.

"Definitely not Earth," I mutter to myself.

I think again of the scene at the Rapid City Airport that in another universe must have happened, getting to baggage claim and being met by Cynthia and the kids. Thomas, who was away at college in Texas during my training but in my vision shows up to greet his old man anyway, turned eighteen two months ago. Kaitlyn is sixteen and has just gotten her driver's license. Bobby is thirteen and into comic books and video games. It is Bobby who sees me first as I exit the secure area and head for the specified baggage carousel.

"Dad!" he exclaims and leaves his mother and siblings behind to rush at me. Bobby is on the autism spectrum, and he and I have always had a special bond. We'd never been apart for more than a week, so the two month separation would have been difficult for him.

The rest of the family catches up by the time Bobby has given me his hug and pulled away. He's normally one to avoid any kind of physical touch, so the enthusiastic, if brief, hug is an indicator of how much he missed me. I take Cynthia in my arms and tell her how much I missed her. Thomas and Kaitlyn envelop the two of us in a group hug as Bobby stands near, debating whether to join in or not.

A sob escapes my lips as the vision fades. Cynthia and my kids are gone, so long ago and so far away that I wonder if they ever existed at all. Then the crying, the mourning, begins in earnest. Our two story house in Box Elder is gone. Box Elder is gone. South Dakota is gone. Everything I've ever known is gone.

"I'm sorry," I blubber to Cynthia, and it occurs to me that she never missed me. That other me, the "real" me, lived out his life with her and with the kids. And then the kids all lived their lives, and then whatever grandkids I had did the same. How many grandkids did I have?

"None," I say out loud. I'm just an eighteen year old kid with the memories of some long dead 48-year-old man. I've been lying in a pod with IVs and feeding tubes for all of my short life, until today. The guy whose memories I have, Kevin Stiles, isn't me. I must convince myself of that.

And yet, I vividly remember watching Thomas walk the stage to get his diploma just this past May. Cynthia and I found him afterward in the crowd. I hugged him, the smell of his shampoo filling my nostrils.

"Congrats son," I had said to him. "I'm proud of you."

"Thanks Dad."

I shake my head and push the memories aside. They are from another life, thousands or even tens of thousands of years ago. And it occurs to me that I have no idea how long this version of the *Armstrong* has been hurtling through space.

"Alexis," I say, "what year is it now on Earth?"

Jordan told me once that calling the on-board Artificial Intelligence Alexis, which is close to the old Amazon Alexa, was his little nod to Jeff Bezos, a friend of his for a while a few years ago.

"Unknown," the female sounding AI voice replies.

"Unknown? Why is it unknown?"

I wait a few seconds, but there is no answer.

"*Alexis*," I say, probably with some irritation in my voice, "why is the current year on Earth unknown?"

"The *Armstrong* has been traveling through space under inertia with no power. There was no way to run a clock, so there is no way to determine how long it was traveling."

I don't know why it matters to me. Even if we are at the pre-programmed destination, one of six planets depending on which iteration of the *Armstrong* this is, I'm still well over a thousand years removed from everyone and everything that the original Kevin ever knew.

"Alexis, can you use the record of past power-ups and the ship's telescopes to examine our last known trajectory and estimate how far from Earth we are and, therefore, what year it might be on Earth?"

"That will take some time to calculate. Please stand by."

I sit at the console looking at the planet on the large view screen. There is a lot of green on the surface, and I wonder what kind of living things are down there. I could grab the mouse and look through the menus to see information and footage from the probes sent down to the surface, but I don't want to take any CPU cycles away from the current task. Besides, there will be time for that later. I have nothing but time.

"Earth is approximately one point seven million light years away," Alexis finally says, "so the current year is estimated to be between three billion one hundred four million seven hundred twenty-three thousand two hundred forty-two and three billion one hundred five million one hundred fourteen thousand six hundred seventy-six."

The small console screen displays the numbers as Alexis reads them.

"What the fuck?" I say.

5

The slowly rotating planet remains on the large view screen as I contemplate the numbers on the console: 3,104,723,242 — 3,105,114,676 CE. Those numbers are ridiculous. I almost laugh at the CE letters. If 3.1 billion years have passed, I seriously doubt that we're still in the "current era". I can't help but wonder if Earth is still even there.

"Alexis, can you still see Earth?"

"No, we are much too far away for that."

"Can you see our sun?"

After a period of silence, I ask again, "Alexis, can you see our sun?"

"Unknown."

"Alexis, why is it unknown?"

"There appears to be a red giant star where Sol should be."

Shit.

"Alexis, could that red giant be Sol?"

"It is possible. Likely, even."

Silence reigns throughout the ship. Earth is gone, burned up and swallowed by a dying star. It can't be. None of this can be real. This has to be a joke.

"All right," I say in a loud voice. "Very funny Jordan! You can come out now. Joke's over."

I stand up and start to walk back the way I'd come, forgetting that my legs are so weak, and I fall forward, my face hitting the floor because my arms aren't strong enough to brace me.

"Fuck!"

I spit blood onto the textured rubber floor. Rolling over onto my back, I gaze up at the ceiling and feel my nose. It hurts but doesn't seem to be broken or bleeding. I have bit my tongue and have to turn my head and spit out more blood. It runs down the corner of my mouth. When the blood enters my ear canal, I sit up.

This can't be a joke. I'm naked and malnourished and weak while looking impossibly young. And my once circumcised penis is now uncircumcised. Jordan could not have done this despite all his money. I am a clone, and I am in deep space with no hope of ever seeing Earth or any other human being other than Linda ever again.

I climb to my feet, more cognizant of my weakened state this time. I find the closest restroom and rinse my mouth out repeatedly until my tongue stops bleeding. Just like everywhere else here, there are no towels, paper or cloth. I don't even want to think about why that is.

Looking at myself in the mirror reminds me that this is no prank. I sigh and then begin the trek back to my room, forgoing my plan of walking around the entire wheel section.

Linda is curled up in a ball sleeping on the plastic pad where I had awakened. I had forgotten that I had moved her here after her little accident. I had cleaned that up, so I could go lie down in her pod. But Linda looks cold in that fetal position, shivering just a bit. Were there supposed to have been blankets covering us that met the same fate as our clothes? I don't know. I climb over Linda and lie down behind her, my body against hers to generate warmth. She doesn't stir.

Closing my eyes, I try to sleep, but my brain won't shut down. A million things run through my mind. I keep telling myself that none of this can be real. Maybe it's all a dream, and I'll wake up back home in my bed with Cynthia beside me. The last thing I remember before waking up here on the Armstrong was the memory retrieval lab. Maybe I can will myself into waking up back there.

"How was it?" I asked.

Linda sighed and closed her eyes. We were sitting next to each other at breakfast in the San Francisco Hyatt Regency where the crew had been staying for the past week since returning to Earth, courtesy of Jordan Walker. Two months of training, both here on the ground and on one of the *Armstrongs* in orbit, had seemed to fly by. At some point, I had stopped thinking of Linda as Dr.

Bascombe as we got to know each other well enough to be on a first name basis.

"It was not pleasant. But at the same time, it wasn't unpleasant. It just was. They say that in a near death moment, your entire life passes before your eyes. It was like that. And it was like a long deep sleep where I dreamt of everything I ever did, everything that ever happened to me. It all just flashed by like it was on its way to somewhere else."

"Well," I said, "it was, wasn't it?"

"I suppose so."

"How long did it take?"

"Mr. Walker's technicians said it was seven hours. But to me, when I was under, it felt like several days."

"Well, I'm only 48 and therefore have fewer memories, so maybe it won't take as long with me," I said with a smirk.

Linda playfully jabbed her elbow into my ribcage. "Shut up youngster."

We both laughed. I took a bite of syrup-soaked waffle and looked at the clock on my phone screen. The van to pick me up and take me to the lab would be arriving any minute. I placed my fork on top of what was left of the waffle and set the napkin down on top of that.

"I guess it's time."

Linda removed the napkin from her lap. "I'll be on a plane on the way back to Fayetteville by the time you're done."

"Oh." It suddenly hit me that I wouldn't see her again. As much as I was ready to get home to my own family, I realized that I would miss this experience with Linda. "I guess you will."

"It has been great getting to know you again these past few weeks," she said.

"Who would have thought when I was sitting in your Anthropology lectures back at the U of A that we would wind up participating in something like this?"

"Life is strange sometimes."

My phone vibrated on the table, and I saw a text from the van driver on my screen.

"I guess that's my cue."

I grabbed the phone and stood up. Linda stood with me and hugged me before I could get away.

"I suppose we'll see each other out there," I said, motioning with my head toward the heavens.

"We'll never know if we do," Linda said. "But we can keep in touch online."

"Yes!" I agreed. "Take care."

I walked out and found the van in the loading area of the hotel. The ride to the lab was so short that I could have walked there in not much more time than it took to ride over in the van.

"Here you go," the driver said as he stopped in front of the main entrance. "Go in, show your ID at the desk, and take the elevator up to the eighth floor."

I had, of course, already toured the facility, but I did as instructed, the security guard in the lobby barely saying two words to me. The elevator ride was quick, and Jordan met me as I stepped out.

"There he is, the man of the hour."

"I heard it takes a lot longer than an hour," I said to him.

"You've been talking to Dr. Bascombe."

"Yeah. She said it seemed to take a lot longer than it actually did."

Jordan shrugged. "It varies based on the individual. The perception, that is."

Since I was scheduled to fly back home as soon as this memory procedure was finished, I was ready to get it over with. "Let's do this thing then."

"All right."

Jordan walked with me to the extraction lab. The preparation for this was something like getting ready for a surgery. I didn't have to get undressed, but I was hooked up to an IV which would be used to administer the drugs that would knock me out. A plastic and metal hood went over my head with electromagnetic contact points at strategic locations on my skull. Those locations had already been mapped during a preliminary test. Once I was unconscious, a large syringe would be inserted into my brain stem, and within that syringe would be the stimulus that activated my memory recall. Everything there would be recorded through those contact points.

"Are you ready Mr. Stiles?" the lead technician asked.

I took a deep breath, thinking, *no, I really wasn't,* and said, "Yes."

The tech injected something into my IV drip, and the world faded away.

I don't remember the feeling that Linda had described, of my life flashing before my eyes as the memories seem to be sucked away. Maybe she just imagined that. For me, everything is a blank after the IV drip started. Until I woke up here just a short time ago. That IV drip started on a place an impossible distance from here, eons and eons ago, on a body that is not this one but only shares a DNA sequence. But it's the very last thing I remember from Earth.

How am I supposed to sleep with this knowledge? Three billion years. The *Armstrong* was never supposed to go that long and that far. What if the shakes we drank no longer have any nutritional value? What if none of the stored food does? We won't live very long then. The only solace I take from that is that in our current malnourished states, it won't take us long to die.

And yet, we both survived this long as we were "grown" in our pods, so there has to have been something of value in what were were fed, intravenously I assume. So why am I worrying about all this? Whatever will be will be. Doris Day's voice singing "Que Sera, Sera" fills my head. There are no molecules left of Doris Day or of the planet where she lived. I'm the only being left in the universe who ever knew she existed.

Stop thinking and go to sleep, I tell myself. Linda moves slightly against me, and I'm tempted to drape my arm over her and hug her to me. However, I don't want her to wake up since I need to get to sleep myself. But my overactive brain won't let me...

6

Linda pushes me away, and I am startled awake. I didn't even realize I'd gone to sleep. I look down and find that my erection is poking her lower back. She pushes at me again.

"Sorry," I say, rolling away from her and onto my back. "This is awkward."

Of course, Linda has no way to know how awkward it is, having no previous point of reference. I can feel that I didn't sleep enough. The lights in the *Armstrong* have been on the entire time. I remember Jordan talking during training about putting those lights on a cycle that matches the days and nights of whatever planet we wind up at. I'll have to tell Alexis to do that before we lie down to sleep again.

I hear the flow of liquid just before the sound changes to that of it hitting the plastic pad.

"Stop!" I yell, jumping up and over Linda.

Linda's body goes rigid, and I see her eyes squint as she starts to wail.

"I'm sorry."

I pull her off the pad and half carry and half drag her to the lavatory. Her urine flow has stopped, which is good. I sit her on the commode and step back.

"This is where you do that."

She sits, still crying, looking at me with such hurt in her eyes. I switch to my soothing voice.

"I'm sorry. It's OK. We're learning as we go, all right."

Linda quiets down, but she just sits there, not peeing. I'm thinking that I should give her a demonstration, especially since I very badly need to pee myself. But I don't want to pee in the shower as she sits on the commode. She might think that the shower is where that is supposed to happen. I also don't want to have her pee on the floor while I'm doing so into the commode, but I decide to risk that anyway.

"Don't go until I get you back up here," I tell her as I pick her up and sit her on the floor in front of the sink.

Normally, I'd pee standing up like any regular guy, but I know Linda will need to do so sitting down. My morning erection has subsided enough that I am able to sit on the commode somewhat gracefully. So I sit and make a big deal out of letting her see and hear my urine flow hit the water below. I hold my finger up to her, imploring her to wait until I get her back onto the commode. Once I'm done, I stand back up, flush, and set her back onto the commode with a grand gesture toward her vulva.

"OK, now you go."

"Baaa," she says and just sits there.

I sigh. "Ah, the joys of potty training a newborn in an eighteen year old body."

Linda continues to look up at me, and something in her eyes reminds me of the 62-year-old version of her that I got to know during training. How could someone so brilliant be reduced to this? Linda, whatever she lacks now, can apparently read my emotions and begins to cry again.

"No no no, it's all right," I say, stroking her head.

She stops crying but looks back down.

"I'm going to keep talking to you like you understand me, OK? Even though you don't." She looks back up at me. "You'll learn the language faster if I do."

I crouch in front of her so that we are face to face. My genitals touch the cold rubber floor and remind me that I'm naked. I ignore it and continue in the crouch.

"Kevin." I pat my chest. "Kevin." I say it with my mouth open, hoping she will see the way my tongue makes the sounds.

"Ka," Linda says.

"Yes, Kevin." I nod in encouragement.

"Ke."

"Kevin."

"Kev."

"Close enough. We'll get to multi syllable words eventually."

"Kev."

"Yes, I'm Kevin. And you…" I point to her. "You are Linda."

"Da."

"Linda." I put emphasis on the first syllable.

"Lin."

"Yes! Linda."

She smiles at me, and I feel as though we've accomplished something even though she still hasn't peed in the commode. Perhaps she got it all out in the pod, which reminds me that I have another mess to clean up.

"Lin," she says to me.

I point back to her. "You're Linda."

I hear the urine stream hit the water in the commode, and I smile and clap.

"Yes. Good job." I can't believe I'm cheering on an eighteen year old for using the toilet.

Linda smiles. When I'm happy, she seems happy. There is an intelligence there even if she can't yet talk or walk. Except that I'm not really happy. I just act that way. I'm using Linda's education as a distraction from the terrible reality we are living.

Since we both got urine on us while lying in the pod, I decide that a shower is in order. I pull Linda to her feet but hold her away when she tries to put her arms around me.

"No, I want you to stand up on your own. If I can do it, you can do it."

"Kev," she says.

"I'm right here. I'll catch you if you start to fall." I just hope I'm strong enough to catch her.

I withdraw my left arm, and she leans hard against the right. I grab her upper arm, pushing back, keeping her upright.

"You got it."

"Huh," she grunts.

Gradually, I relax my grip on her arm. Linda sways from side to side but doesn't fall over. My hand flattens, with only my palm touching her. I slowly pull the hand away, and Linda remains standing.

"See," I say in an excited voice.

Linda laughs and seems proud of herself. I lean into the shower stall and turn on the water.

"You're doing so good," I say as I get the water temperature right.

I take Linda's hand, and we step into the cramped shower stall. She leans against the wall but remains upright. I wash my hair, rinse, and then wash Linda's. She cries when shampoo gets into her eyes, and I point the shower head right at her face.

"I'm sorry," I say over the sound of the water. "I seem to take a lot of things for granted, as if they should be common knowledge."

Once we are all clean and rinsed, I turn the shower off. We stay in the shower stall for a few minutes as the water drips off our bodies. The stall is not big, and we are standing so close that we are touching in several places. My body is eighteen years old, which means my hormones are also eighteen years old. The entire reason for this mission is the propagation of the human species. Jordan said it over and over during our training. So I know, intellectually, that Linda and I will have to enter into a physical relationship in order to conceive the children that will advance our species. But my feelings for her now are entirely paternal. She's naked and beautiful, but she's helpless like a child. She has no idea what's going on or why we are here. Even though Linda has no idea what it means, I am ashamed of my arousal, so I turn away from her and step out of the shower stall, still damp.

"Kev," she says, still leaning against the wall of the shower stall.

I look at her over my shoulder so she can't see my arousal.

"It's all right. I just need a minute."

Linda pushes off from the wall, takes a step out of the shower stall. She almost falls, but catches herself, arms out away from her like a walker on a tightrope. I turn around then, ready to catch her if she falls. Linda appears not to notice my almost erect penis. Maybe I'm worrying about it too much. She makes a muted laughing smile as she looks at me, as if she's proud of taking her first step. I laugh with her as encouragement and then motion for her to take another step toward me.

"Come on. You got this."

The smile fades from Linda's lips as she concentrates on moving her foot forward. She reminds me of a very old movie I saw in a film class, Boris Karloff as Frankenstein's monster walking stiffly in boots that seem too heavy.

"See! I told you!" I keep that excitement in my voice, and Linda laughs again.

"We get this walking down, and then we just have to get you talking." *And potty trained*, I almost add, but even I don't want to think about that.

Speaking of potty training, I realize I'm going to have to go soon myself, and since I don't remember seeing a bidet in any of the bathrooms on board, it's time to test those vacuum packed toilet paper rolls I saw earlier.

"Lin," I say. She looks up from the floor after having watched each of the five or six steps she has made. "I need to go check on something. Do you want to walk with me?"

Motioning up the corridor, I nod my head, and she nods along with me.

"We'll walk slow."

And we do walk slowly, making our way through the remaining pods. At one point, Linda tries to look through the plastic canopy of the one with the dead child, and I steer her away. She won't understand what she's looking at, I think, but I can also see her getting highly upset at the sight. I'm going to need to figure out what to do with the remains. I've got so much to do and to worry about, but right now, Linda's care and training has to take a priority.

When we arrive at the supply area, I realize how hungry I am. One of those shakes from earlier doesn't sound good at all. There has to be something else to eat here. Of course, I haven't been all the way around the wheel section yet.

"First things first," I say, but Lin remains quiet.

I pull one of the cube shaped multipacks of toilet paper rolls down from the shelf. It's large but not large like the toilet paper packs in the grocery store since this is vacuum packed so tightly. I find the seam and rip, halfway expecting the paper rolls to disintegrate into a cloud of dust. But they don't. Toilet paper expands and rolls bounce out, going every which way. Linda laughs, probably at the expression on my face more than the toilet paper going everywhere. The ends of the rolls seem to be glued, so at least the paper isn't streaming out everywhere. I pick one of the rolls up and examine it, breaking the glued seal and unrolling it a little. The paper is rough, more like the toilet paper in a public restroom than the soft stuff one would buy for home. But it's perfectly intact and useable. The only difference between it and the ones that had been left in the restrooms is the vacuum packing.

"It's got to be the zero g," I say to Lin.

She gives me a quizzical look.

"Think about it. This and our clothes were in zero g for three billion years. They're made of fibers. Without gravity, those fibers drifted apart. Maybe they all did OK for the first thousand years. Maybe the first million years. But eventually, they all drifted apart. I mean, how could you test something like that? Put a roll of toilet paper and a t-shirt in zero gravity for three billion years, and see what happens? You can't. I mean, you could. We did, essentially. But no one knows we did." I didn't add that there literally was no one around *to* know we did.

Lin still looks at me with that same expression. I look back at her and give a slight laugh, trying not to sound like I'm losing my marbles. Part of me wonders if anyone thought to vacuum pack some clothes, but that's a minor concern. We can just be naked, especially as I'm teaching Lin how to use the commode. When all three kids were little, Cynthia and I let them run around naked which helped a lot with potty training.

The major concern I now had was for the parachutes in the landing module. They are pressure packed, but are they pressure packed enough to counter the effects of zero g? Most of the outside of the EVA suits are plastic, but parts of the arms and legs are covered with a tough canvas-like cloth. Is that still intact, and if not, is it integral to the suit's integrity? Theoretically, we could live up here, train, and go to the planet's surface without ever having to do an EVA. But what if something came up, and one became necessary? How would I know if the suit would protect me without trying it in the airlock? And if it didn't work, would I have enough time to get the airlock closed up again before either suffocating or roasting or freezing depending on where the sun was shining?

I don't want to spend time worrying about things I can't do anything about at the moment. We are going to be on the *Armstrong* for at least a year and maybe longer. That's the plan anyway. We could stay longer than that though. We have provisions for six people, and there are only two of us.

I'll work on those problems later. Right now, we need to take care of necessities.

"Come on Lin," I say, moving onward with the roll of toilet paper still in my hand.

7

I have decided to call my companion Lin rather than Linda if only to distinguish her from my memories of Linda back on Earth. Lin is what she calls herself, after all. I'm going to have her keep calling me Kev even after she graduates into multi-syllable words. I can't explain why, but I want to distance ourselves from our original persons. I don't even want to say the word selves now, even though the memories of the training still seem like yesterday.

Lin walks almost as well as I do now, which isn't that great to begin with because I still feel malnourished. When we walk past the control room, Lin, in a voice filled with awe and wonder, says "Ohhh" at the planet on the large view screen.

"I'll show this to you later." I take her by the hand and lead her through. The next room is a dining area with a table and six chairs, next to a galley with a stove and oven and cabinets full of metal pans, dishes, and utensils. After the galley should be the hydroponics area where, I hope, all kinds of fruits and vegetables are being grown. I'm afraid of finding empty trays with nothing but dust, and I stop to prepare myself. Lin looks at me, her head cocked to one side.

"The next room is where our food should be." I point in that direction. Lin looks that way then back at me. "If there's nothing in there, we may starve to death."

She looks back toward the hydroponics room and then starts forward. I take a deep breath and walk alongside her. My knees almost buckle at the relief I feel when I see all the green leaves under the UV lights.

"Thank God," I say.

Linda steps forward and gently touches one of the leaves.

"That's a squash plant."

I walk between the hydroponic tables marveling at the display of tomatoes, green beans, corn, and other vegetables. There's even a watermelon plant. The multitude of robotic arms hanging from the ceiling had been taking care of planting, watering, cultivating, and harvesting the vegetables. Jordan had said that he didn't expect regular seeds to last more than three thousand years even frozen, so he had sequenced the DNA of each plant and cloned them in a procedure that seemed as complex as cloning us. Except that only two of the six of us had survived the cloning process. I take a quick inventory of the plants and don't see either carrots or potatoes. Did those not survive the cloning process? I had never been a fan of carrots back on Earth, so I doubt I will miss them much. But no potatoes means no French fries or potato chips or mashed potatoes and gravy.

The 3-D printers at the other end of the room look to be in working order. I know there are protein filaments stored in the cabinets underneath the printers. I look in one of the freezers past those 3-D printers and see several newly printed steaks and hamburger patties. I take out two steaks and leave them on the counter to thaw. Lin walks over and presses her finger into one of the steaks.

"I have to cook them first." I take her hand and lead her to the next room which is another storage area for tools and heavier equipment. There is also an airlock and two EVA suits. I open the first cabinet and look at the suit. It looks perfect from the outside, but that's all plastic and metal. The elbow and knee joints are made of what looks to be canvas covered in some kind of plastic coating. Those look intact. I detach the helmet and look inside. All the head padding that I expect to see is gone. Just for fun, I set the helmet on my head and feel how uncomfortable it is.

"Uh," Lin says, wanting to put it on her head.

I take it off and hand it to her. She takes it and sets it on her head and removes it less than three seconds later, handing it back to me and then rubbing her temples where the unpadded protrusions in the helmet sat.

"Yeah," I say, setting the helmet on the floor and removing one of the gloves.

The plastic fingers seem to be all right on the outside, but when I hold it upside down, a pile of fuzzy dust falls out onto the floor.

"Let's hope we don't have to do any space walks," I tell Lin, knowing that she'd have to be at least competent with the airlock controls if I were to ever go out. Either the suit would merely be extremely uncomfortable because just the comfort padding had disintegrated, or an EVA would be deadly because the disintegration affected something vital to the suit's function. There are other EVA suits in the service module, but they are the same model as these, and they have been in zero-g the entire trip.

I laugh out loud, and Lin gives me a questioning look.

"I was just thinking that the suits in the center section have been in zero-g longer than these were, and then I thought, these have only been in gravity for twenty years or so, not even a drop in the bucket compared to the three billion years the *Armstrong* has been out here."

Her questioning look remains, and I shrug. "I know, it's not funny, really. Maybe I'm losing it. And it's only the first day. Or second depending on how you count that sleep we had, a nap or an overnight."

If I'm remembering correctly, the next room past this garden and food generation and storage area is the first bedroom, my room to be exact, so I turn around, taking Lin by the hand, and lead her back to the galley. Thankfully, the grill and the microwave both seem to be working. I talk as I work, defrosting the steaks and chopping several yellow squash I find in the fridge. Cooking had been one of my — Kevin's — pastimes back home, so I know my way around a kitchen. I grill the steaks medium rare, just hoping this 3-D printed stuff tastes at least good enough to eat. There are onions in the fridge, and I slice one and cook it with the squash.

"Smells good at least." Lin just stands silently watching.

"Squash," I say, holding up a slice before dropping it in the pan.

"Wash," Lin says.

"Squash." I pronounce it slowly with my mouth open so she can see how I form the sounds.

"Kawsh."

I laugh. "OK, maybe I should have started with an easier word." I turn my attention back to the grill. "That is steak."

"Teak."

"Steak."

"Steak."

"Very good!"

Lin laughs with me. She seems to have mastered walking far faster than I had expected, and if she has Dr. Bascombe's intellect, even without her memories, I am hopeful that she will be talking very soon. Once we sit down and eat, I am pleasantly surprised at how much this steak tastes like the real steak I remember from Earth. I cut Lin's steak while chewing my first bite, careful to avoid the spot on my tongue where I bit it. I don't want to take the time now to teach her how to use a steak knife. Once I slide her plate in front of her, she picks up a cube of meat with her fingers, sniffs it, and then pops it into her mouth.

When she appears to be trying to swallow it whole, I grab her hand and say, "No, no, no. You have to chew."

I demonstrate by chewing a cube of steak with my mouth open so she can see. She mimics me, chewing with her mouth open.

"Good," I say, thinking that this is no way to instill table manners. *Just keep her from choking to death and worry about table manners later. Or not. There's nobody but us here.*

After dinner, I take Lin to the nearest restroom, just in case she needs to go. She stands looking at the commode, a blank look on her face.

"Do you need to potty?" I ask.

"Potty."

"Yes, potty." I point toward her pelvis. "Do you need to go?"

She remains standing and expressionless, and I realize with a bit of dismay that I have to go. I sigh.

"Fine. I need to go. Maybe if you see me do it, you'll know what to do."

I sit down and go, watching her face crinkle as the smell hits her.

"Ooo," she says.

"It's normal."

But I reach back hit the flush lever anyway. I let her watch me wipe. I should talk her through that too, but since she doesn't understand, I don't. It feels a bit humiliating to do this in front of her, but I don't know of any other way to make her understand. And hell, we're already naked all the time anyway, so I can't come up with a good reason other than personal humiliation for giving her a demonstration.

When I've done and flushed again, I motion for Lin to sit. She does, but she just looks up at me. I'm reminded of the worst struggles of potty-training Bobby, my youngest and the one on the autism spectrum.

"Stay there."

I motion for her to remain where she is, and I walk back to the galley to clean up from dinner. I barely get everything to the sink before I break down, falling to my knees and crying, thinking about home and family and how this is all there's ever going to be, just Lin and me. There can never be any rescue, no homecoming, no happy ending. We are stuck here at this planet, whatever it holds for us.

Quit feeling sorry for yourself, I tell myself after a few minutes of despair. *You've still got a lot of work to do if you ever want to get off this ship and down to the wide open spaces of the planet below.*

But I still want to go home. I want to take Cynthia and the kids camping in Custer State Park or to watch the Wild West shows in Deadwood. I want to hold Cynthia in my arms and breathe in the scent of her shampoo. Knowing that those things are gone forever makes me want them even more.

I bury my face in my hands to try to stifle the sound of my sobs. I don't know why. The only other person in the universe who can hear this won't understand. I let the tears flow.

I jump when a hand touches the top of my head, and I fall back on my butt. Lin stands over me, a look of concern on her face.

"You scared me," I say to her.

Lin stands still, just looking at me. I wipe my face with the back of my hands and rise to my feet.

"Did you go potty?"

Lin smiles. "Potty."

"Let's go see."

I motion for Lin to lead the way back to the bathroom. I can tell by looking at her backside as she walks that she didn't wipe very well. Back in the bathroom, I help her with that, talking her through the proper procedure. Lin's body is the same age as Thomas, my oldest. The thought just occurs to me as I feel more like her parent than anything else, helping her and teaching her.

"We have to think of each other as family now, you know."

Lin just grunts as we wash our hands.

"It's just you and me. No one else." Unless, of course, we create another person, which was Jordan's aim. But I can't even think of that now. How am I supposed to be Lin's parent and then, later on, be her lover?

I want to study up on the planet below, but how can I do that with Lin always around, always needing me? We walk to the lounge area and sit on the floor in front of the thing that used to be a couch.

"Alexis, turn the screen on."

The view screen on the wall brightens but doesn't display anything. Does it work? And even if it does, will the digital files still be intact? Lin looks at me, her expression questioning as it seems to be most of the time. I want to find something educational for her to watch, but only one thing comes to mind.

"Alexis, play *Sesame Street*."

I expect that it will start with something recent, but apparently, the *Armstrong* has every season of *Sesame Street* in its memory. Images of kids playing on an urban playground, the cars in the background from the early

1970s, appears on the screen, the theme song of the show accompanying the video. Lin laughs with delight. I want to cry at this glimpse into a world that is long dead. And yet, it feels like yesterday that I was in that world. The unreality of our situation hits me again. The computer said three billion years has passed, and yet, the digital storage is intact enough that the video is playing without a hitch. I want to scream out at Jordan to stop this, that his joke or his experiment is in bad taste. I have to know if this is real and not a very expensive simulation. But how do I do that?

8

I stand to my feet. Lin tries to follow, but I motion for her to stay seated.

"Watch the show. I put it on for you."

From her knees, she looks from me to the view screen and back to me.

"I'll be right back."

I motion for her to sit, and she does. Walking backward, making sure she stays where she is, I head to the control room next door. The image of the planet is still on the control room view screen. It's supposed to be a video feed from a camera on the service module which isn't turning like the wheel section is. But is this a live video feed? It could just be a recording of an AI-generated planet. I could be in a large facility on Earth, part of a Jordan Walker-funded experiment. That's what it could be, an experiment. He's put too much money into it for it to be a mere practical joke. But I need proof. I can't be over a million light years from Earth. I just can't be. I was in San Francisco only a day or two ago. I should never have agreed to let people working for Jordan put me under anesthetic.

Short of opening the airlock, what can I do to prove to myself that any of this is real? I look at the planet on the screen. The clouds inch along as the planet turns in its rotation. I can stop the wheel section from spinning. If I'm really in space, we'll go to zero gravity. There's no way to simulate zero gravity in an Earth-bound facility. Of course, Jordan has six of these in Earth orbit. Or at least, he said he did. We only saw one of them during training. But he couldn't control the experiment if I were really on the *Armstrong* that's in Earth orbit. No, if we're really in space, then this has to be real.

I sit at the console and use the keyboard to bring up the page for controlling the wheel section spin. We had gone over the procedure just last week during training, so I find the page without any problem. The spin is creating 0.941 gravity force. The AI is supposed to be programmed to emulate the gravity on whatever planet we wind up at. I make a mental note of that number and then lower it to zero. That should activate the air thrusters and slow the spin of the wheel section. If we are actually in space, that is.

I leave the screen up and hurry back to Lin. She's going to freak out if she starts floating, not that I expect that to happen. Lin smiles when she sees me, pointing at the screen, and saying "Cookie!"

"Ah yes. Cookie Monster. One of my favorites."

It doesn't take long to feel the effects of the slowing rotation. The feeling of motion makes me a little nauseous. Lin gives me her questioning look again.

"Sorry," I say, "but I had to be sure."

Lin and I both find ourselves floating up from the floor. Before we get too far away from it, I straighten my legs and push off toward one of the windows. When I look out, I see the planet below as it has been appearing on the control room view screen. I look around the edges of the window, trying to find evidence of another video screen mounted there. We are really in space, that much is certain. The window looks like every aircraft window I've ever seen. This is all real, the planet, the three billion years, all of it. Lin and I *are* clones. I had so hoped this wasn't real, that I could go home eventually. Now, there is no hope. We are here. We can never go back to Earth. There isn't even an Earth to go back to, even if we could somehow survive the three billion years it would take to get there.

Three billion years! And yet, the data storage seems intact. The view screens work. The camera displaying the shot of the planet below seems fully functional. This mission could be compiled into a commercial for all that stuff except that there's no one left to sell to. The thought makes me laugh out loud. Lin laughs with me as she floats toward me. Her eyes seem drawn to my mid section for some reason. As she nears, she reaches out and pushes down on my penis which has been floating up in the zero gravity.

"Lin!" I grab myself before she can touch it again. "That's wildly inappropriate."

She continues to laugh as she looks down at herself, but stops laughing when she realizes that we are built differently.

"I can't have that talk with you until you start understanding the language."

Her face returns to that familiar questioning expression. I let go of my genitals, which have received more blood flow than I'm comfortable admitting, and take her hand.

"We need to turn the gravity back on."

I use my feet to push us away from the wall with the window, heading roughly toward the control room. We float to the corridor wall where the zero-g handles have been placed, and I push us to the console. I get Lin into one of the seats. There are no seatbelts, and even if there were, they probably would have disintegrated with the clothes and loose paper products. Lin immediately starts floating up and out of the chair as I take my place and toggle the wheel rotation to return to 0.941 gravity. The air thrusters aren't very powerful, so the return to gravity should be gradual. But I feel the pull to the outer wall of the wheel, what becomes the floor when the spin creates gravity, almost immediately. Lin's body seems to settle back down to her chair. I hear the pots and pans clanging about in the galley. I had left them in the sink without washing them. They floated up when I turned the gravity off and are now crashing back down.

I feel silly. The idea that Jordan would create an experiment like this on Earth was ludicrous. But with that idea completely debunked comes the realization that our situation is hopeless. Lin and I are here, and there is no going back. And yet, that desire to go home is so strong with the memories seeming so fresh. Lin reaches over and wipes a tear from my cheek. I wipe my other cheek.

"Sorry. I don't mean to be so emotional." She still has that questioning expression with everything I say. "I envy you. You don't even know what we've lost."

She points past me, toward the lounge, and says, "Cookie!"

"See. Cookies. We don't have any. And we don't have the means to make any. So you'll never know what Cookie Monster was so crazy for."

Lin still looks toward the lounge, so I take her hand and rise from my seat. I take a quick look at the console and see that the wheel spin has us at 0.89 gravity, so the air thrusters should shut off in a few more seconds.

"Let's go watch *Sesame Street*."

9

It takes me the equivalent of a week to pull myself out of my depression. We spend the time eating, watching old educational shows on the lounge view screen, and cleaning up from my impromptu zero-g test. There is a proper procedure to follow, and I didn't do it. Water from the commodes had floated up and then splashed down onto the lavatory floors when the gravity spin resumed. Plants and dirt from our garden had also floated up and then made a mess. We start our clean up efforts with the garden, sweeping up the dirt and putting it back in place, harvesting what vegetables we can, and replanting what still needs to grow. It takes us a while to clean up the galley and the lavatories. When the tasks seem overwhelming, the weight of it makes me want to just shut down and do nothing. I cook our meals and sometimes clean the dishes after eating, and I try to make sure Lin is beside me so that she sees what to do. The third time we sit down to eat, she sees me cut my own meat and tries to grab a knife to use on her food. But she grabs it by the blade and cuts three of her fingers. Luckily, the cuts aren't deep, but the only thing I have to treat the wounds are alcohol and paper towels that had been vacuum wrapped. The gauze and stitches that had been in the first aid kits have disintegrated.

Lin spends most of her time in front of the view screen while her fingers heal, like a typical twenty-first century kid. She holds a wadded up paper towel in her hurt hand for three days, but I manage to get her to give it up after the cuts scab over. I have Alexis set most of the interior lights on the *Armstrong* to turn off for nine hours out of every twenty-four, so we can measure the days or cycles or whatever we want to call them. It occurs to me that the old Earthbound measures don't mean anything anymore. How long is a day on the planet below? How long is a year? The AI on the *Armstrong*, having been in orbit for almost twenty Earth years now, has collected and computed all the data to answer these questions, but I haven't found the motivation to ask her. I guess I'm not ready to let go of Earth.

After seven cycles, I finally get tired of being tired and start an exercise regimen. Lin and I have put on a little bit of weight from the meat and vegetables we've been eating, so it's time to make sure that weight gain goes into the right places. Thinking that a workout will help me sleep, I start an hour before our lights out period begins, on the stationary bicycles. Lin watches me for a couple of minutes before climbing onto the one next to me and just sitting there.

"Here," I say, "you have to enter a preset time and difficulty."

I lean over and set hers for ten minutes at the easiest setting.

"Now you pedal."

I resume my routine, letting her see how I do it. She watches for a moment, and then starts pedaling, slowly at first and then picking up speed.

"Fun, isn't it."

We bicycle for a few minutes before Lin abruptly stops and climbs off her bike.

"Watch Sesame Street," she says, rubbing her quads.

"Burns, doesn't it. No pain, no gain."

Lin turns and heads for the lounge. She has made a lot of progress throughout the week, fully potty trained now with only one more accident after the zero gravity debacle. I've been letting her have more independence, but I watch her enter the lounge area. The curve of the wheel section of the *Armstrong* isn't so bad that I can't see into the next room. She disappears from view when she sits on the floor in front of the ruined couch, which has become our spot for watching shows. I wish we had something to use to cover the couch so that we can sit on it.

My bicycle routine has another thirteen minutes, so I keep pedaling until the clock runs out. When I dismount from the stationary bike, I move over to one of the resistance machines. My legs are sore from bicycling, but I can work on my upper body. I sit with my back to the machine and start with chest flies to work my pectoral muscles. On Earth, Kevin was never a big gym rat, but he had worked out sporadically throughout his life. I have to start at a very low resistance setting. There just isn't much strength in my body right now. That is going to have to change. I just need to get off my ass and get into this gym thing every day.

I'm in the middle of my second set of chest flies when I hear Lin's scream. I jump up and rush to the lounge, berating myself for giving her this much freedom when she still knows so little. Lin stands between the shredded couch and the view screen on which Big Bird and Mr. Snuffleupagus are in deep conversation. When Lin sees me, she holds out a blood covered hand.

"Bud," she cries, remembering the word blood from her accident with the knife.

"What did you do?" I ask as I look at her. When I see blood on her thighs, I relax. "It's OK. Let's get you to a potty."

We walk to the nearest restroom, my hand gently on her shoulder. I get her seated on the commode.

"I'll be right back." I use my soothing voice. "Everything is all right. I just need to see if I can find any tampons."

I run over to the storage area, hoping that whatever feminine hygiene products we had were vacuum wrapped and didn't disintegrate. I find the right cabinet, which is stuffed with vacuum packed cases of tampons. Each one is in a plastic sleeve, and each sleeve is in a box within the pack. I pull one down, the velcro coming free with a ripping sound. When I get the seal broken, I pull one of the boxes out. The paper box doesn't fall apart, which is a good sign. I take the one box back to the restroom with me. Lin is calmer than when I left her.

"Okay, I don't have much experience with these. Only one of my kids was a girl, and she always had her mother to help her with these kinds of things."

I open the box, pull one out, and rip open the plastic sleeve. Inside is the hard plastic covered tampon. I shake it up, and no dust falls out of it. The tampon inside looks to be intact. I sigh in relief.

"OK, so you insert this end inside and then pull this plastic piece out. The tampon stays in with this string sticking out." I make the motions as I say this, hoping I don't have to insert it myself.

Lin looks at me with a dull expression, her hand over her abdomen like she might have a stomach ache. I hold the tampon out to her, but she doesn't take it.

"This is supposed to absorb the blood, so you don't leak it out everywhere."

"Bud," she repeats.

"Yes, blood. It's totally normal. You're a woman, and this… This is just something that women have to go through every month."

Lin doesn't understand much of what I'm saying, but I feel the need to explain it anyway.

"You see, your body prepares itself for pregnancy, and when you don't get pregnant, it's got to clean itself out every month and start over. Understand?"

She shakes her head no.

"That's all right. You don't have to understand everything now."

"No bud!"

"I know. I don't like the sight of blood either. Actually one of the most successful horror writers in history started his career as a novelist with a scene kind of like this, eighty-something years ago. A girl having her first period and didn't know what it was." I pause. "Well, I guess it's been a whole lot longer than eighty-something years ago now."

I have never had to insert a tampon, but it looks fairly self explanatory. Rather than do it myself, I place the tampon in Lin's hand and then guide her hand to the necessary spot. I have to take her other hand and spread the labia a bit to get it inserted.

"Now, push that plunger thing, or whatever it is."

I push with her finger on it and then pull out the plastic applicator.

"You leave the string hanging out so you can pull it out when it absorbs as much as it can. And you throw this plastic thing away." I toss it into a trash receptacle. "How does it feel?"

Lin looks at me with a dull expression.

"Does it feel OK? If not, we can take that one out and try another one. We have plenty. There were supposed to have been four women on this mission."

Lin continues with the blank look.

"Well, let's stand up and wash our hands. And your legs."

After washing up, I walk with Lin back to the lounge, but she keeps going.

"You want to go lie down?"

She nods, and I escort her to her bed. We've been sleeping apart since I turned up the thermostat after the zero gravity experiment. When Lin lies down, I lean over and kiss her forehead. It was the kind of automatic thing Earth Kevin used to do with his kids whenever they had any kind of traumatic or tough experience. And that's how I feel about Lin, like she's my child. Physically, we're the same age, but mentally and emotionally, I'm way ahead of her. That's ironic since Earth Linda was fifteen or so years older than Earth Kevin. I also know that, eventually, I'll have to take Lin as a lover if we are to propagate our species, which is the sole objective of this mission. Will I be able to switch from paternal love to sexual love? Even though the hormones are raging in this eighteen-year-old body, and I'm jerking off a couple of times a day just to relieve the pressure, the thought of sex with Lin turns my stomach. She needs me to be a parent, so I'm being a parent. Will I even be able to transition from parent to lover?

I turn and walk back past the lounge, ordering Alexis to turn off *Sesame Street* as I walk by. I have to get off my ass, quit feeling sorry for myself, and get to work. Lin needs more than an outdated children's TV show for an education. I resolve to sit down and start school with her the following day.

10

Before I go to bed, I sit at the console and start looking at the planet below. It looks like Earth until I really notice the shape of the land masses. I pull up a geological map compiled by the *Armstrong's* artificial intelligence on the small console screen. There are three main continents all surrounded by water, only one of which straddles the equator. A host of islands dot the oceans in various spots. The two poles are covered by small white spots. The planet doesn't tilt nearly as much as Earth did, so the changes between seasons are minimal. It takes twenty-three hours and fourteen minutes for the planet to turn a full rotation, similar to an Earth day. Its orbit around the star is three hundred and twenty-two planetary days, making a year here a couple of months shorter than I'm used to.

The planet has three moons, the largest of which is about one and a half times the size of Earth's moon. The other two are similar in size to Luna. The smallest one appears to be the largest from the planet's surface due to the proximity of its orbit, about 175,000 miles from the planet. The other small one is about 300,000 miles away while that largest moon orbits at almost a half a million miles out.

Upon the *Armstrong's* arrival in orbit, forty landing probes were sent to the planet's surface. The map I'm looking at shows that only twenty-three of those are still functioning. Most of the defunct seventeen were in coastal areas. The tides are erratic and occasionally extreme depending on how the three moons line up. A schedule of those tides has been compiled, but I can't sense any definitive pattern. One probe that had landed far enough from the shore to survive but near enough to measure tidal patterns had recently measured extremely high tides four times in the span of thirty-two days and then none for the next three hundred. The difference between the lowest tide and highest tide can be between four and fifteen miles planet wide, depending on the depth of the ocean near the shore.

The temperatures on the surface are generally warmer than on Earth. One of the probes about two thousand miles south of the equator has measured a twenty-year high of fifty-one degrees Celsius with a low of ten degrees Celsius over that same span. Living all my life in the United States, I am used to seeing temperatures in Fahrenheit.

"Alexis, from now on, convert and display all

temperatures to Fahrenheit," I say.

The numbers on the screen change instantly. That particular place had never gotten below fifty degrees Fahrenheit but reached a scorching 124 degrees on at least one occasion.

"Sounds like Phoenix," I say, except that rainfall is abundant, with most days seeing at least a half an hour of steady downfall.

The daily averages at that particular probe show a high of 93 degrees Fahrenheit with a daily low of 78 over the course of those twenty years. That seems tolerable to human beings, especially human beings who don't own any clothes.

It occurs to me that I should give this planet a name. I don't want to keep thinking of it as "the planet". I turn on the camera feed from the probe that had sent the weather statistics I had been looking at, and the video of the planet from orbit is replaced on the large view screen by a forest scene. The trees tower over the probe, so much that I wonder how the solar panels (could they be called "solar" panels if the star shining on it was not Sol?) are able to get enough light to keep the probe powered on. I take control and toggle the camera around to see light rippling off the surface of a small lake. It all looks so idyllic that there's only one thing I can think of to name the planet.

"Eden."

I sit back and watch the sun begin to set across the lake. I've always been an outdoor person. Or at least, Earth Kevin was. It's still difficult to convince myself that he wasn't me, because of all his memories in my head. He moved his family to South Dakota for all of the outdoor activities there: Custer State Park, Badlands National

Park, Devil's Tower over in Wyoming, Spearfish Canyon, and the Black Hills. The thought of remaining cooped up on the *Armstrong* for two more years instead of being out in the open, feeling the sunshine and breeze on my body, is depressing. But I still understand the plan Jordan implemented and the need for it. Lin and I are in no shape to start living off the land. We can barely walk a lap around the wheel section of the ship. And I must take the time to study Eden to determine the best landing spot for us. I'm going to need Lin's help, and for that, she has to be educated. None of that will happen overnight.

If anything, I'm now mad at myself for essentially wasting the last week even though I tell myself that it doesn't matter. There are only two of us on a ship that is equipped for six. Theoretically, we could stay up here almost ten years, although I might be insane by then.

The video of the lake suddenly goes blank, and I sit up. The live data on the small console screen freezes, and I realize that between the rotation of the planet and the orbit of the *Armstrong*, I've lost the line of sight to the probe. I press a few keys, going back a few screens to the list of probes sent to Eden's surface. Selecting one that hadn't transmitted in many years, I bring up a list of saved videos. Jordan had said during training that the *Armstrong's* Artificial Intelligence would evaluate and decide which videos to save and which to discard to preserve storage space. I play the most recent video, which doesn't display a date but an age. This video was taken over fifteen years ago. It shows a vast flat plain of dark brown. There is no plant or animal life to be seen, only dirt or mud or whatever it is. On the horizon, I see a line of white. The white seems to move and pulse, and behind it I begin to see blue. The water rushes toward the probe, covering what looks to be several miles in less than two minutes. It hits the probe with enough force to pull its anchors from the ground and send it rolling in the tumult. The video comes to an abrupt end, freezing on an image of a cloudless blue sky.

"OK. Stay away from the coasts. Got it."

For some reason, an old country song that I haven't even heard since I was a kid pops into my head, "Ocean Front Property in Arizona," and I have to laugh. I consider pulling up more videos from the surface, but the lights are going to dim soon, so I push away from the console and head toward bed.

11

I try to project a more positive attitude the following morning. Lin and I shower together like we've done since waking from our induced coma, but this time, I merely supervise as she cleans herself. We could continue showering together. We are naked all the time anyway, and there's nothing sexual going on. But I want her to be independent, able to take care of herself in case anything happens to me. We eat a breakfast of strawberries and 3-D printed bacon that is nowhere near as good as real bacon.

"I hope they have something like pigs on Eden," I say.

"Pigs," Lin repeats.

"Yeah." I scrunch my face and pull the end of my nose up. "Oink oink."

Lin laughs, and for just a moment, I see a hint of Dr. Linda Bascombe as she used to be on Earth. I remember the first meeting of all six crew members in Jordan's board room in San Francisco. Jordan had just gone over the idea of the mission, the cloning and memory upload processes and how the probes to the planet and the transport craft we would use to go to the surface all worked. Jordan had paused and looked at the five of us.

"Any questions?"

"Oh my God, yes!" Dr. Bascombe said, and we had all burst into laughter.

I push the memory away before the anger and sadness consumes me again.

"Oink oink," Lin says, pushing the end of her nose up.

I can't laugh, but I do give her a smile. She seems to sense my struggle with melancholy and ends her pig imitation, taking a bite of fake bacon.

After we finish eating and cleaning up, I take her on a walk around the wheel section of the ship, completing four laps. I have to pull her away from the lounge every time we pass it. After the fourth lap, we stop in one of the lavatories so she can do her business. I help her change her tampon.

"You have to start doing this by yourself, OK. You know where the new ones are, and you've helped me put them in. You should be able to do it by yourself now. OK?"

"K," she repeats.

We walk over to the fitness center, and I show her how to do bench presses. I start off with what I think is a low weight, but I can barely do one rep. So I lower that weight and manage eight reps. Lin lies down on the bench when

I get up and proceeds to do ten reps before wearing out, unable to push up that eleventh time.

"Show off."

Lin laughs at the expression on my face. I get back on the bench and do twelve reps this time, stopping after the twelfth rather than continuing until failure. It's better to pace myself in this body that has never seen serious exercise before. I'll need to make sure Lin paces herself as well, which probably won't be a problem as she seems to have lost interest while I was doing my second set and has wandered toward the lounge.

"Lin, we aren't done working out."

She looks back at me before sitting down in her regular spot on the floor in front of the shredded couch. I march to the lounge and stand over her.

"Lin, we have to build our strength. We can't just sit around watching TV."

She points at the screen. "Cookie," she says in a fairly good imitation of Cookie Monster.

I shake my head. "No. Exercise first, then TV."

"Cookie!"

I shake my head. "No. Come exercise." I step toward the fitness room and motion for her to follow me.

"Cookie!" Lin screams at me.

I continue to shake my head no as I walk back to the machine. Lin has the mind of a toddler, I tell myself. I can't make her exercise; I have to make her want to exercise. Hopefully, she'll realize she has to do this first if she wants to watch *Sesame Street*. I lie back down on the bench press and do another set.

"Cookie!" Lin screams again, making me lose count of my reps.

I sit up after what I think is ten and say in a loud voice "No!"

After a moment, Lin jumps to her feet and storms toward me. I point to the bench press.

"Exercise."

"No!"

She brushes past me and heads toward her room.

"Fine," I say like an irritated parent.

I continue my workout, thinking that I'll let Lin pout. I do a complete chest and shoulders workout, but with very light weights and high reps. I don't feel much of a burn like I remember from Kevin's workouts on Earth, but at least I'm working the muscles. When I'm done, I go to the storage area and make myself one of those tasteless protein shakes that we had right after waking up. I move a couple of the cans of protein mix to the galley to be in proximity to the rest of the food and dishes. The workout and making and drinking the shake takes me over an hour. I haven't seen or heard anything from Lin during any of that time, so I head toward her room to check on her.

As I approach her "room", I see that she's on her bed with her legs spread apart, her hands at her crotch with her fingers fluttering like the wings of a hummingbird. My first instinct is to go stop her, to tell her that masturbation out in the open like this is not appropriate, but I stop myself. Who is here who would be offended, other than me? And do I want to make Lin feel shame? God knows I've done a lot of jerking off this week myself although I've managed to do it in private when Lin is either asleep or otherwise occupied by Big Bird and Burt and Ernie. I can't approach her anyway as seeing her this way has affected my own hormonal eighteen-year-old body, so I back away, careful not to make any noise.

After taking care of myself at the nearest restroom, I head back to the control room with that big image of the planet Eden on the large view screen and sit at the console. What do I do now? I know nothing about raising a toddler in the body of a sexual adult, especially one who will some day become my lover. Because if she doesn't, the human race will die out again, and this mission will have been for nothing. But I just cannot bring myself to consummate that until Lin knows what it means, and she needs a lot more education before that happens. It would feel like taking advantage of her. And when Lin becomes more cognizant — "grows up" for lack of a better term — she might think that as well. So I will wait, ignoring all these raging hormones in my body. How did I, or Earth Kevin, ever make it out of adolescence with any semblance of sanity?

Another reason for my hesitancy is Cynthia. I know that she's long, long gone, and as much as I am distancing myself from Earth Kevin, I still feel married to her. I look down at my hands, and the lack of a wedding ring should convince me that I'm not married to Cynthia and never have been in this body. Lin is obviously in need of sexual release or fulfillment, so part of me says, go ahead. No one will ever know besides Lin and myself. There are no other people left to judge us, to judge me.

"There's God," I say out loud.

But is the God of humanity really way out here? The *Armstrong* hurtled away from Earth at a half a million miles an hour for over three billion years. Is God really that big? Or did he travel with us? Earth Kevin always considered himself a Christian with a deep belief in God.

Did I still share that belief, or did my current situation prove that God was just a construct of human beings, a way to explain what we otherwise couldn't?

"Are you still there?" I won't call it a prayer, but I am talking to God. "It seems hard to believe that you could be. Our solar system is apparently gone. Lin and I are so far removed from everything we've ever known that we can't even fathom it, from the standpoints of both distance and time. According to the Bible, we were supposed to have a thousand years of peace at the end times. One thousand years. Sounds like a blink of an eye compared to how long we're separated from everything. If you did create this entire universe and not just the small part of it that we were in, then you are unfathomably big. I don't know how to reconcile that."

I take a deep breath, my eyes on the planet Eden on the view screen in front of me. Its rotation is apparent but still slow. I am watching the terminator from day into night when I see a silver triangle hovering high above the planet, standing out in the light from the star, with the blackness of space behind it. I lean forward and then stand up, walk around the console, get as close to the screen as I can without the image distorting. The triangle looks smooth with no visible markings or indentions. It hovers, unmoving, for what seems like several minutes but was probably much less before suddenly zooming away with no visible sign of any propulsion system. I stand, dumbfounded, watching the spot where the triangle had been, but it doesn't reappear.

No physical object could have moved as quickly as that triangle did, so, therefore, it couldn't have been a physical object. Maybe it was a trick of the light on the camera lens. That seemed to be the best explanation. But what if it wasn't a trick of the light? What if it was made by an intelligent species and could appear to defy the laws of physics? But there had been no evidence of any advanced civilization on Eden, no lights at night on the planet surface, no artificial satellites in orbit (other than the *Armstrong)*, and no signs of any sentient creatures from the cameras on the surface. That last thought reminds me that I need to go through the catalog of animal life on Eden that the cameras have picked up. I also don't know anything about any other planets in this star system. Might any of those others be a home to intelligent life advanced enough to build that disappearing triangle?

Just before seeing the object, I had been talking to God. Could the triangle have been a sign? It was three sided, like a trinity, as in the Father, the Son, and the Holy Spirit.

"Shut up," I say out loud.

I am reading too much into what was probably some kind of optical illusion. If God is here and really wanted to give me a sign, it would be something more obvious than a fleeting glimpse of a UFO. I watch the spot where the triangle had been for several minutes before setting an alarm for 23 hours from now to remind me to come back tomorrow and look for it again. Maybe whatever it is, a trick of the light or an actual spacecraft, has been a daily occurrence, and I just haven't noticed it before now. Even if it was an alien, should I even be worried about it? The *Armstrong* has been in orbit here almost twenty years with no interference from any aliens yet. At least, that's what I'm telling myself.

12

I am able to find a wealth of resources on the *Armstrong's* computer for teaching language skills to children. It's almost as if Jordan anticipated that not all memory downloads would work as designed. I find a slide show to help with Lin's vocabulary since that seems to be a good starting point. We'll start on the alphabet and the sounds each letter makes after she is able to communicate better. At least, that seems reasonable. I know nothing about early education. We sent our kids off to elementary school for all that stuff, although they were, of course, able to talk well before going to kindergarten. It seemed like it took a long time to get them there though. Before we moved from the Dallas area to South Dakota, we often visited Cynthia's parents in Wichita Falls. When Kaitlyn was little, she used to call it "Witch Stop Falls" instead of Wichita Falls. In our family, that forever became the new name of the town, Witch Stop Falls.

Thinking about Earth Kevin's family hurts too much, so to think of something else, I navigate to the files of verified animal life on Eden. Lin rushes into the control room before I can even get the first video file open. She has blood all over her fingers and a trickle of it running down her leg.

"Did you not change your tampon?" I say.

She shrugs her shoulders, her long hair frizzy and hanging in front of her face which is flushed from either embarrassment or exertion. I doubt that she even has a concept of embarrassment, so it must be exertion. I stand and motion for my chronic masturbator to follow me.

"Let's get you cleaned up."

A newly cleaned up Lin and I return to the control room, and I pull up the slideshow of items on the big screen. The first ones are simple shapes.

"That's a square."

Lin looks at the shape on the screen with the word "square" displayed below it and back at me.

"Square." I say the word slowly, letting her see the way my mouth moves.

"Care," she attempts.

"OK, maybe a q sound wasn't the best to start with. Square."

"Quare."

"Good. Now say the S sound. Ssss-quare."

"Square."

"Yes!" I point to the screen. "That's a square."

"Square."

I click to the next slide and say, "Circle."

Lin smiles, catching on as if it were a game. And I'm sure I'm repeating some of what's she's already seen on *Sesame Street*. "Circle."

"Good job."

We go through slides of several shapes before coming to one of a tiger. I start to say the word and then stop. She may never see a tiger in her life. I doubt that Eden has the same species of animals that Earth had. I think of a Tyrannosaurus Rex and certainly hope that it doesn't.

"Tiger," I say.

"Tiger."

The next slide is an elephant. Lin tilts her head at the image, probably thinking of Mr. Snuffleupagus, the wooly mammoth on *Sesame Street*. Are there elephants on Eden? If not, I don't see why I should be going over words that she will never need to use, so I click ahead several screens, past the animals, until I come to a picture of a car, a Toyota Camry from, I think, the early 2040s. It occurs to me then that Lin is never going to see a car in her lifetime either.

"Everything has changed," I say. "These things will never mean anything to you."

Lin looks at me, her eyebrows raised, and points to the screen.

"That's a car."

"Ka?"

"Car."

"Car."

"Yes. That's how we used to get around back on

Earth."

"Earth?"

"Yes. That's where we are from. Neither of us has ever been there, of course. But I still have memories of it. Memories implanted into my head." I point to my temple.

Lin gazes at me, a serious expression on her face.

"Sorry," I say. "It just hit me that from here on out, nothing will be like it ever was before. And I thought I could teach you different words, get you talking sooner. But these are things that you'll probably never see. So I'm at a bit of a loss."

Lin gives me a forced smile, as if she's pretending to know what I'm saying. And maybe she is getting at least a sense of it. Linda, Earth Linda, was extremely intelligent and perceptive, so it seems natural that her clone would have some of that already built in. I take a look around the room.

"Let's do this instead." I pat the desk that we are sitting behind. "Desk."

"Desk."

"Yes." I point at the small console, touching the screen. "Monitor."

"Montor."

"Close. Mon-i-tor."

"Mon-i-tor."

We make a day of walking around the ship, me naming every item I can think of, and Lin naming them back to me. When we come back around to the control room, I point at the screen on the console.

"Do you remember what that is?"

Lin takes a moment to think before spouting, "Mon-i-tor."

"Very good!"

Lin smiles and laughs, proud of herself. And she should be. After going through dozens of words, remembering one of the first ones like that is impressive.

"I like to see you smile," I say.

"Smile," she repeats.

"Yes." I point to my mouth. "Smile."

She points to her mouth and repeats it.

"Well, that's your mouth. But what your mouth is doing is a smile. Like, see, this is a frown." I give her an exaggerated frown, point to my mouth again, and say, "Frown."

"Frown." Her mouth curves downward.

"There you go. But this is your mouth." I point to mine and then hers.

"Mouth."

"Yes. And this is your nose," I say, pointing.

"Nose."

"And these are eyes."

"Eyes." Lin reaches forward and almost pokes me in one of them.

"Whoa, you have to be careful with eyes."

As soon as I say it, I recall a day when I was doing a similar exercise with my youngest, Bobby. He had succeeded in getting a finger into my eye, and I had recoiled. He's started crying immediately, thinking that he had hurt me. I took him in my arms to comfort him, telling him, "It's all right. You just have to be careful with eyes."

I take a deep breath, trying to keep from crying at the memory. Why does any little thing keep reminding me of what I will never see again?

"Frown," Lin says.

I laugh in spite of myself. "You are too smart for your own good."

Lin tilts her head, as if she's in deep thought. *Stay in the here and now*, I tell myself. "That's enough education for one day. You want to watch *Sesame Street*?"

Lin gives me a vigorous nod.

"All right then. I'll go put it on for you."

While Lin is distracted by *Sesame Street*, I gather the trash to eject it into orbit via a special airlock. Most of the receptacles we use have been full or nearly full for a day or two. I also take the opportunity to remove the remains of the crew clones that didn't survive. I start at Stacey's pod, getting the canopy open and feeling the top of the plastic mattress. I don't see or feel any remains, so I move on to Kacey's. She was still in a fetal stage when her clone died. I'm expecting some kind of odor, but there's nothing when I open the canopy. Wishing I had gloves, I pick the body up and dump it into the bag. There is a crusty bit still on the mattress that I am able to peel off.

I feel a little bad, treating the bodies of my former crew members as trash. But the fact is that they lived full lives on Earth and have been spared this existence. Lilly Markum's clone's remains are as big as a five-year-old child, but they fit into the large trash bag with ease. Her body easily separates from the mattress, and I don't have to scrape or peel anything off. I'm going to scrub all of these mattresses down later.

Jordan's clone requires a new bag as the first one is full, and the body had made it to at least early adolescence and is therefore the largest of the remains. I grab the body by the shoulders, lifting it and trying to pull it into the bag, but the body breaks in two at the waist in a cloud of dust. The organs, red, brown and crusty, are visible at the break.

"Yuck," I say as I slide the upper half into the trash bag. The bottom portion goes next, pieces of it flaking off at my touch. I'll have to run a vacuum over this mattress before scrubbing it down.

The garbage airlock is small and located on the floor between the control room and the galley, the thinking being that most of our garbage will be generated in the kitchen area. I have to eject one bag at a time, and the process takes about three minutes for each bag. There is a compacter inside that condenses the bag into its smallest possible form. The container then decompresses before opening into space. The interior wall snaps forward as if released by a spring, pushing the square of trash out toward the planet. The trash will orbit for a few rotations before succumbing to the planet's gravity and burning up in its atmosphere.

I say a small prayer before jettisoning each bag, commending the bodies and whatever spirits might have inhabited them to God.

"All right Jordan," I say from one knee as the second bag, the one with his clone's remains, is ejected, "it's just Lin and me now. I doubt this is what you had in mind, but here we are."

I pull myself to my feet, intending to finish cleaning those pods but now feeling suddenly exhausted. Instead, I join Lin for a classic episode of *Sesame Street*. Cleaning can wait.

13

The creature on the screen sniffs at the camera. It walks on four legs, is covered in gray scales, and has a long snout full of very sharp looking teeth. The measurements displayed on the screen list its length as twelve feet long, standing at a height of about three and a half feet on all four of its legs. The thing's feet appear to be webbed. *It looks like a cross between an alligator and a giant salamander.*

This is, thankfully, the most fearsome looking creature I've seen in the video files shot by the various landers sent to the surface. Most of the animals I've seen have either scales similar to this creature or plain skin. The only fur-covered animals I have seen are the ones near the two poles. Given that Eden is generally much warmer than

Earth, the lack of fur makes sense.

Of the twenty-three still functioning probes, only four have drones that are still flyable via remote from the *Armstrong*. I switch to a live feed of the drone attached to the probe that had recorded the alligator-salamander creature and use the keyboard to fly it around the area. I point the camera up, looking for any kind of flying creatures. I see something moving in the distance, so I fly it that direction. The drone locks onto the nearest creature, giving me the distance and the approximate size. Its wingspan is over nine feet. The closer the drone gets, the more I can make out. It's not a bird. It looks something like a cross between a bat and pterodactyl, arms hanging below them with long claws that look more like fingers than talons. The faces of the creatures are short and stubbed, like that of a bat, but the wings are made of a thin but tough looking membrane. They are all blue in color, blending in with the sky. I'm amazed I was able to see them through the camera lens of the drone. I surmise that they are day hunters given their color camouflage. Is that color flat, or can they change color to blend it with their environment? I switch to an infrared view and see that they are warm blooded creatures.

I turn the drone away before one of the creatures decides to get curious and point it back toward the lander. This gives me a nice panorama of the area. A river with a flood plain that is at least ten times as wide as the current flow of water is just a few miles away. I'd like to check it out. The power on the drone looks good, but the orbit of the *Armstrong* will soon sever my line of sight connection. I give the drone the Home command so that it will fly back to its charging station on the lander even if my orbit takes me out of range before it can get there.

I type a few notes on the keyboard, wondering how I'm ever going to whittle down the list of landing sites. Whichever one I choose, Lin and I will be spending the rest of our lives there, raising children, hopefully a lot of children if our species is to have a chance. There are so many factors to consider. We have to have a viable food and water source. We need a conducive climate, both in temperature and precipitation. We need to know about all the animal and plant life in the region, which animals are predators, and which will be good for turning into livestock. Eden is prone to flooding with its crazy tides due to the three moons. As I could see from the river flood plain, those tidal floods affect the fresh water systems too.

Of course, I have to wonder now how much salt is in the ocean water and how much of that gets moved inland during these floods. Would the water from the river even be drinkable, or would we have to rely on catching rainwater? I have so many questions that I can't process them all. At least I have a lot of time to decide these things. We could live on the *Armstrong* for several years if we needed to. Unless I go completely stir crazy, that is.

I check the time and see that it has almost been a full day since seeing the triangle. I've had Alexis adjust the clocks to reflect a "day" on Eden. Rather than reinvent the wheel, I had her shorten the length of a second so that a day would still be twenty-four hours. That probably violates some rule of time recording, but since Lin and I are the only humans left, the rules no longer apply. In fact, I can make or change the rules as I see fit. I still haven't figured out what to do about marking months and years to match with Eden's crazy moon cycles and orbit around the star. But I have time to figure that out.

I watch the spot on the view screen where the triangle had appeared yesterday. I don't know if I'm hoping for a repeat or not. The *Armstrong's* orbit around the planet is irregular, so the chances that I am anywhere near where I was in relation to the planet at the same time yesterday are slim. But if the *Armstrong* is the subject of the triangle's curiosity, perhaps my location over the planet is irrelevant.

I watch the spot for fifteen minutes, and nothing happens. Perhaps I should talk to God again. That seemed to have prompted it yesterday. I take a deep breath. The sounds of *Sesame Street* filter through from the lounge next door. Lin is fully occupied.

"God, are you still here? Were you ever here? I don't know if the thing I saw yesterday was a sign from you or not. I feel kind of silly talking to you like this. You created Man on Earth. Unless, of course, Man came to Earth from another planet just like Lin and I are doing here. Man, that would open a whole new can of worms, wouldn't it. But assuming the Adam and Eve story is accurate, it seems like you didn't have much to do with creating Lin or me. I mean, Jordan's team of scientists did all the work. I'm a clone. I have all of Kevin Stiles's memories, but does that constitute a soul? Can a clone have a soul? I mean, the original Kevin, who lived out the rest of his life on Earth after that memory upload, he had to have had a soul, right? So what does that mean for me?"

I still stare at that one spot, but nothing happens.

"Was that an alien intelligence, or was it— actually,

that sounds wrong. Lin and I are the aliens here, aren't we. But was that a craft piloted by intelligent creatures, or was it something else? Will I ever know? And will I ever see it again?"

I stop talking, just listening, but the only thing I hear is the sound of The Count talking about the number three coming from the view screen in the room next door. The rest of the ship is quiet. I watch a line of clouds over a mountain range on the planet below. It looks like the Earth I saw while in orbit, training on one of the *Armstrongs*, and yet the images from the surface look so alien. I should correct myself. Earth Kevin was training on one of the *Armstrongs*; *I* was not. I just have the memories of it.

Looking up from the planet, I think I see a flash of the silver triangle near where I had seen it yesterday. But when I look directly at the spot, there's nothing. I scan the entire screen.

"Come back," I say in a soft voice.

All I see is the light of the sun reflecting off the planet. Had I really seen the triangle again? Or did I just want to see it again so badly that my mind made it up? For that matter, had I really seen it yesterday, or was the whole thing a figment of my imagination? Was it a sign to give me reassurance? If anyone ever had reason to question his or her faith that there is a Creator, it is certainly me right now. I keep watching the area for another hour, but nothing happens. With a sigh, I get up and head toward Lin in the lounge.

14

Lin and I have been awake for a month now. Thirty days have passed. We both look much different than we did that first week. I found some scissors and razors, so Lin and I cut each other's hair. Lin cut mine with a lot of direction from me. I shaved my beard off, and I now look like Earth Kevin did at this age. My legs were especially hairy at approximately eighteen years of age compared to how I remembered Earth Kevin's at age 48. So I shaved them too. Lin was so taken by my new look that she insisted on shaving her legs as well. With her new shorter hair style done in a ponytail, she looks more like a twenty-first century Earth woman, albeit a naked one. Her hair now looks like sixty-something year old Earth Linda's did. Maybe I cut it that way on purpose.

Her vocabulary is increasing almost exponentially each day. Like my own kids, she used "me" as the subject of her sentences, as in "Me watch *Sesame Street*," but I got her to switch to the proper "I" within a couple of days. And, thankfully, she finally got burned out on *Sesame Street*. We've spent the last few days watching some old Australian cartoon called *Bluey*, which isn't too bad.

Lin is a very touchy-feely person as was Earth Linda during the mission training. She is always touching me, putting her hand on my arm or shoulder and bumping hips as we are walking laps around the ship. And she seems to crave the same kind of physical touch from me. After completing a task or mastering something new, her responses to my verbal praise, "Good job," or "Awesome!", are lukewarm at best. But if I touch her in some way, pat her shoulder or take her hand in mine, her face seems to light up. It's all innocent, of course, as she has the mind of a child. But she has the body of an adult woman, and I can tell that she wants something but either doesn't know what it is or doesn't know how to verbalize it.

As for myself, I have the raging hormones of a typical eighteen year old male. Sometimes, after physical contact with Lin, I have to go be alone for awhile. Lin is able to correctly identify the name of every vegetable that is growing in the hydroponics room, so I give her a hug while saying, "You are so smart!" When I try to disengage, she keeps holding on to me, laughing all the while. Her breasts are pressed against my chest, and my stiffening penis rises against her pubic mound.

"Hey," I say. "I'm going to need you to let go."

"No. I like."

"Lin." I use my stern voice.

When she lets go, I step away, but her eyes are directly on my now full erection.

"I'll be back." I hurry off to a lavatory and lock myself inside until I get it under control.

I don't know how long I can hold out. It's obvious she wants what she doesn't understand. So I decide to show her the consequences of what she wants.

We are up to ten laps around the ship during our morning walks. Normally, we stop in the fitness center and do some resistance training to build muscle, but today, I pass that room and stop in the lounge. I have moved a couple of chairs from the control room into the lounge so we no longer have to sit on the floor. This required a bit of work on my part since those chairs were bolted down to keep them in place during the eons of zero-g on the *Armstrong*.

"Watch *Bluey*?" Lin asks as we sit.

"No. We need to watch something else. Alexis." I wait for the ding. "List childbirth videos."

Since the primary reason for this mission was propagation of our species, there is an extensive library of childbirth videos for the crew to watch before moving down to the surface of the planet. According to the mission plan, the first children should have been born on board the *Armstrong* during our planned two year stay in orbit after waking up. I look at the list and decide on a normal uncomplicated natural childbirth.

"Alexis. Play number three."

The video starts playing with a narrator's voice telling us to meet Patricia, an accountant from San Diego, and her husband James as they walk into the main entrance of a hospital. Patricia is dressed in a t-shirt and shorts, her large abdomen stretching both. Her hand is on her belly as she walks. The man with her, presumably the father, pulls a suitcase on wheels. The video looks to be at least twenty years old—or at least twenty years old when Earth Kevin underwent his memory upload. I turn and look at Lin as she watches, her eyebrows pulled forward in thought.

"She big," Lin says.

"She's pregnant."

"Pregant?"

"Preg-nant."

"Pregnant. What that?"

"She's going to have a baby."

Lin's eyebrows raise at that. "Baby in her tummy?"

"Yes."

I know she'd seen babies on the shows she had watched, so I don't need to explain that to her.

"How they get baby out?"

"Just watch. They'll show everything."

The video cuts to Patricia in a hospital bed, a belt wrapped around her abdomen with a baby heartbeat monitor, the sound of which fills the room. The doctor, a middle-aged woman in scrubs and a long white coat, comes in and checks Patricia out as James sits beside her. Patricia tenses up as the doctor looks up at a monitor. The mother-to-be grits her teeth and closes her eyes.

I watch Lin more than I watch the video. This was one of many we watched during the mission training back on Earth. Over three billion years ago, I remind myself, even though it still seems like just a few weeks have passed. Lin cringes every time Patricia screams out in pain.

"She hurt?" Lin asks.

"Yes, she feels pain. Having a baby is painful for the mother."

The video progresses with nurses measuring times between contractions and the doctor stopping in several times to check to see how dilated Patricia's cervix is. About fifteen minutes into the video, everything is ready. The hospital gown is moved aside, and Patricia sits with her legs spread and knees in the air. The graphic nature of the scene would have made most people from Earth a bit queasy, but Lin, who had never worn clothes in her life, leans forward and watches Patricia breathe and push, breathe and push.

"You're doing fine," the doctor says more than once.

The father uses a washcloth to stroke Patricia's forehead as he whispers things into her ear. She waves him away when it's time to push again, and it reminds me of how useless I (or Earth Kevin) felt in the delivery room during the birth of each of my (his) kids. With this next push, the top of the baby's head can be seen between Patricia's labia.

"I see the crown," the doctor says after Patricia relaxes. "One more push, I think. But take a few moments."

Patricia nods, and the father resumes stroking her forehead.

Lin leans even further forward, gazing intently at the screen. After a few moments, the doctor says, "OK, one more big push."

Patricia's face contorts as she almost sits up in the bed, pushing for all she's got. The baby's head emerges, then the shoulders, and then all of it slips out into the hands of the doctor. Lin joins in with all the ooh's and ah's in the delivery room. She turns and looks at me, elation on her face.

"Baby!" she says.

"Yes. Watch." I point back to the screen.

She watches as the father cuts the umbilical cord and the baby is held up so Patricia can see him. "Meet your son," the doctor says.

"Oh my God," the father says.

Patricia seems too exhausted to speak. The baby boy is then taken to another station in the room near Patricia's bed.

"OK. I do need one more push for the placenta," the doctor says, but Patricia doesn't seem to hear her. "Patricia."

The father pulls his eyes away from his newborn son and talks softly into Patricia's ear. She raises her shoulder and pushes out a red and purple mass onto a tray which is collected by one of the nurses. Lin's face scrunches up when she sees it come out.

The camera pans over to the baby station where a nurse calls out the weight, seven pounds three ounces, and the length, nineteen and a half inches, all over the sounds of the baby's rhythmic cries. I stop watching the screen before the memories of the births of Earth Kevin's three kids can create a longing that will never be fulfilled and instead turn my full attention to Lin. She rubs her flat abdomen as she watches the baby get diapered and swaddled in a blanket and then handed over to Patricia. The new mother tries to nurse him, and he immediately stops crying to latch onto a nipple. Lin caresses her own nipples as she watches. I resist the impulse to tell her to stop, that rubbing her nipples like that in front of me isn't appropriate. But there's nothing appropriate or inappropriate anymore. Lin and I are all there is, so we can decide those things ourselves. And if Lin does it, then it's fine with me.

"Aww," Lin says as the baby nurses with gusto.

There are other videos of more complicated births in the files, two of Cesarean sections and another of a breech birth, but I decide to wait to show those to Lin. I will be watching them though, knowing that at least the first few deliveries will be solely up to me to accommodate. I am, of course, assuming that there will be several to come. If either one of us is infertile for any reason, this this whole mission was for nothing. We would just live out our lives on the strange planet below and nothing will ever come of it.

"I have baby?" Lin asks as she touches her vulva, pulling the labia apart.

"I hope so," I tell her.

She looks at me, then at my suddenly stiffening penis.

"You have baby?"

"No, I can't. I'm a man. Only women can have babies."

"I'm woman?"

"Yes."

"How I get baby?"

And there it is, the big question. I knew she'd ask after watching the video, but I don't know if I can explain it in words that she can understand. But I had shown her the video anyway? Why? Because I'm horny. I admit it. I'm in an 18-year-old body with all the hormones sharing a confined space with a beautiful naked woman while also being naked myself. How could I not be horny? But I still don't want to take Lin before she is able to both understand and consent. And she can't really consent if she doesn't understand.

"A man and woman have to come together, and when they do, the man puts something inside the woman that makes a baby grow."

"How together?"

I sigh. "I wonder if Jordan put any porn in the video files?"

"Huh?"

I shake my head. "Nothing." Lin looks at me, an expectant look on her face. "Ok, you see we are different?"

Lin shrugs. "Different?"

"You have breasts," I say, pointing.

Lin touches her two nipples with her index fingers and then touches mine.

"We both have nipples, yes. But your breasts are different from mine. And you have a vulva." I point to that part of her body. "And I have a penis." I point to myself.

"You say not touch there."

"Yes, I have said that. Because of what it leads to."

Lin gives me that questioning look of hers.

"Look, when a man and woman love each other, they join together."

Earth Kevin never had this hesitancy to talk to his own kids about the birds and the bees. But then again, he never had to worry that what he was saying might sound selfish or self-serving. And I guess that's what has held me back all these days on the *Armstrong*. I don't want to persuade Lin to do anything that she might regret later and then hold it against me. Of course, the two of us have no other option. I take a deep breath and start again.

"A man would take his penis and put it inside the woman's vagina." I point to the relevant body parts on both of us as I tell her this.

Lin's eyes widen as she gazes at my erection.

"I know. It's a lot to take in." I shake my head, realizing what I just said. "I mean, I didn't mean it that way. It's a revelation. You know. But it feels good for both the man and the woman. And the man shoots things into the woman that make a baby."

Lin's mouth is open as if she's still in a state of astonishment.

"We do that?" she asks.

"Only if you want to."

"I want to."

I gaze into her eyes, looking for some sign that she's sure this is what she wants. She breaks into a smile, and I can't help but smile back. I lean forward and kiss her mouth.

15

I have either created or awakened a monster. Lin wants sex all the time, and I've had to explain to her more than once that a man needs time to recharge in between. That first time, we took things slowly with lots of foreplay. Earth Kevin had never taken a woman's virginity that I know of, and I wanted to be careful with Lin. After we had finished, Lin curled up against me on the floor of the lounge and wouldn't allow me to let go of her. We slept there until the lights went out, at which point, I picked her up and carried her to my bed. It was only later that I noted with some satisfaction that I was now strong enough to carry her a fair distance through the ship.

The following morning, Lin woke me up by grabbing my penis and saying, "Again?"

Still groggy and with sleep in my eyes, I said, "Sure."

For the first time in three weeks, I missed my regular time in the control room to watch for a return of the silver triangle. That triangle had never reappeared as far as I had seen, but I still try to keep an appointment there every day at that same time.

Lin's period arrived the second day after our sexual awakening, but that only seemed to increase her libido.

"It's going to be yucky," I told her.

"We shower," was her reply.

Just to make things easier, I took her to the largest shower on the *Armstrong*, in what would have been Jordan's room, of course, and we did it there.

After a week of this, Lin has become my shadow. No longer content to watch her shows on the view screen in the lounge, she is with me almost all the time. This makes it easier to get her to do regular exercise. We've cut back on the cardio since we've been getting enough of that from sex, but she has taken to resistance training. She makes a big show of flexing her biceps and getting me to feel them. She's probably hoping that such contact will lead to more sex, but I'm starting to get more strict on enforcing our schedule. Lin does sit with me in the control room watching videos from the planet's surface with me.

Alexis, the *Armstrong's* Artificial Intelligence, has chosen three possible landing sites for us based on climate and livability, but I'm looking all over the planet. The animal life varies widely from place to place, and I want a good idea of which species would be dangerous to us and which might be good to eat. There are weapons in the cylinder section which we can take to the surface, but the ammunition for those weapons is, of course, limited. No weapons were stored in the wheel section where we would be living before our descent to the planet just in case members of the crew didn't do well psychologically. I have to laugh now as I recall Jordan's speech about the rationale for that.

"We are going to wake up and realize that we are just clones, that we are billions of miles from Earth, and that everyone we ever knew is dead. Those things are going to put us under tremendous emotional distress. We therefore need to store the weapons, weapons that we will definitely need on the surface of whatever planet we're at, some place difficult to get. If they are in the cylinder section, someone would have to turn off the gravity spin in the wheel section to get to them. And you can't do that without everyone else knowing about it."

The fact that Lin and I are the only ones who survived and that my memory download was the only one that worked has only added to my emotional distress. The good news is that I'm too much of a coward to even contemplate suicide. Not that I'd need a weapon to do that as long as I could get into the airlock. Besides that, I'm too curious about what living on Eden will be like. And there's no way I would ever leave Lin alone.

I shake my head and get back to the task at hand, looking at possible landing sites, wondering why a random thought about weapons started me thinking about suicide. There is a site on the southern continent that looks promising. It sits in a valley of a mountain range about thirty-five hundred feet above sea level. The temperatures there are mild, with an average high of 91 degrees and a low of 73. The camera on that lander stopped working about six years ago, and the drone is non-responsive, so I can't pull up a live feed of any kind. But there are a multitude of video files stored in the *Armstrong's* system to watch. I check the historical stats. The highest temperature recorded there in almost twenty years is 106 Fahrenheit; the lowest is 53 degrees. It rains one out of every three days on average with an average annual rainfall amount of 42 inches (and that's with a shorter year than on Earth). The highest recorded wind speed during those years has been sixty-four miles an hour during a thunderstorm that also dumped eleven inches of rain, also a record for a single day. That storm happened eight years ago, so there should be video of it.

"Watch something?" Lin asks, her hand caressing my arm.

"Yes, we are going to watch another possible landing site."

I click on the first video in that lander's folder, and a video of a jungle landscape fills the large screen. Lin's hand grips my arm at the sounds of chirping and cawing echoing across the valley.

"What that?"

"I don't know. This is a recording, so I can't pan around and look."

We look for any movement in the plant life which is plentiful and looks like a mix between high grass, palm fronds, and ferns, but we don't see anything. A section of the sky is visible, and I watch it, hoping to see any sign of movement, wondering if those blue camouflaged bat things are also on this southern continent.

"Waaa!" Lin says, pointing at a small cat-like creature with smooth looking green skin.

"Great, more camouflage," I say.

The cat thing has four legs and long pointed ears, much longer than a cat from Earth. It is small but bulky with what looks to be a lot of muscle mass.

"I wonder if they'd be good to eat."

"Eat?" Lin looks toward the galley, and I realize that we are late for our mid day meal.

"Yeah. We're going to have to eat something down there."

The long whiskers on the animal's snout is what gives it that cat like appearance more than anything else. I stop the video and look at Lin.

"You want to eat?"

She smiles and looks down at my lap. "We sex first?"

I laugh. "Sure. Why not."

16

Life progresses on board the *Armstrong*. I have set up a calendar to mark the time. Since a day on Eden is fairly close in length to a day on Earth, I'd had the computer ever so slightly shorten the length of one second so that twenty-four hours matched a day here. Years on Eden were 322 of those days though. Should I split the year into ten months of 32 or 33 days? On Earth, a month matched the lunar cycle. The word "month" itself was a variation on the word "moon". With three moons around Eden and the lack of seasons due to just a tiny wobbling on the planet's axis, how should I split the year up? I decided on a simple year-dot-day notation. We are now at 1.56 if I count the date 1.1 as the day Lin and I woke up. After typing 1.56, I look at it on the console screen.

It seems too short to convey a date, but then again, we haven't been awake very long. And it reminds me of the star dates in the *Star Trek* movies and TV shows, although those dates were always inconsistent and didn't make much sense if you tried to create an actual timeline of events. Maybe I'll go back to using month names when we get down to the planet. And maybe I'll start the whole calendar over again when we get there since that is the ultimate goal. Everything will begin again when we are finally on the ground.

I go back through the log I have been keeping, inserting those short dates where I remember them and guessing where I don't, so that I have a decent chronology of everything that's happened so far. Most days are fairly boring. Things like, "Lin learned the words console, computer, and control room today," or "We ate fake bacon that was bland and green beans that were crunchy and tasty," make up the bulk of the log. When I think that I should be keeping better records, I also think, *Who is ever going to look at this?* But then maybe I'll find myself in a situation where I need to look at what has happened before and what we've done before, to address some new problem. So I make a more detailed report for today.

Lin and I walked four laps, did three sets of chest presses and chest flys, engaged in intercourse on the resistance machine. We then watched videos taken from Lander 14 from eleven, eight, and seven years ago. Observed three species of animals near the lander, the green cat-like creature, a long eight-legged serpent looking thing, and a large creature that resembled something between a deer and a horse, although hairless like most of the animals on this planet. We then switched to Lander 7 which still has a working drone with camera. Caught site of the blue camouflaged bat things again. One of them dove before the camera got near and snatched a small rodent-like animal from the ground and flew away with it.

That seems adequate, but it makes me wish I had been doing this more thoroughly all along. I need to make a decision on where to settle. There are three landing craft in the command module, or center section, each designed to carry two people to the surface. These landing craft are also designed to be used as dwellings once on the surface. I plan to send one down to the planet before Lin and I go, to test both the heat shield and the parachute. The latter is my main worry given what has happened to the cloth and paper products here in the wheel section. Those parachutes are packed under pressure, so I'm hoping that the effects of three billion years of zero-g have been minimal. I don't know what I'll do if the chute fails to open and the landing craft crashes. Would we just live out our days up here, eating whatever we can grow? There are supposed to be rocket thrusters under the craft once the heat shield is jettisoned, and I remember flying it to an almost soft landing without a chute in a simulator. But that was a simulator, and I only did it successfully twice after crashing four times.

I never wanted to be an astronaut. The idea of being cooped up inside a small spacecraft for long periods of time never appealed to me. But I watched a lot of movies about astronauts, and the one thing they always had was Mission Control. I not only don't have a Mission Control; I don't even have a home planet. And even if I did, it would take over a million years for any message to get to it. A million years! That used to seem like such a long time. And it still does when I think of the here and now. But the *Armstrong* hurtled through interstellar space with my frozen DNA for a million years, and then another million and another million, over three thousand times. Recorded human history is only about five thousand years or so. At least it was when my memory of it ends. I can't help but wonder how long it lasted.

I have so many questions that will never be answered. Is the speed of light unattainable for a space craft as Jordan thought, or did human beings find a way to break through that limit? Jordan had said that in the unlikely event humanity did break the speed of light barrier, they would come and either retrieve or destroy the six *Armstrongs* that were launched in the third quarter of the twenty-first century. The fact that I am here leads me to believe that they never did break that limit. But if they did, did humanity expand to other planets before Earth became uninhabitable? Even if they did create a way to travel at the speed of light, it still would have taken them over a million years to get where I am now. And that's only if they went the right direction. Did human civilization even last a million years? We'd only made it just over five thousand before we developed the means for completely destroying ourselves, so I have no reason to believe that we lasted even close to that long. Even if we did last a million years, the human species still will have been extinct for over three billion years. The numbers stagger me the more I think about them, and the more utterly alone I feel. Yes, Lin is with me, and I thank God for her. At this point though, I've come to think of her as a part of myself. I guess, in that way, we are married.

One good thing about not having a Mission Control is not having someone pester me about my health. I don't have anyone monitoring my heart rate, blood pressure, respiration, etc. I need to start doing that myself at regular intervals, for both Lin and me. We had a mission plan, of course. There were tasks that each of the six of us were supposed to accomplish every day of the two years we were in orbit around the planet. I have just had trouble finding the motivation to do any of it all by myself. That was one of the things that I remember Earth Kevin having trouble with; whenever the workload seemed to be overwhelming, he had a tendency to just shut down. That's what I've done. I've shut down. I have done just enough to get by. Sure, I've been teaching Lin the language, but that's more so I'll have someone to talk to than anything else.

"I tired," Lin says, walking over from the lounge where she had been watching a documentary about Africa.

"Yeah, I'm tired too."

I leave the log up on the screen and take Lin's hand. Locking my workstation screen had been instilled in me from Earth Kevin's working days, so it took me a little while to give it up. Why lock the screen when there's no one in existence other than Lin and me to get into the computer?

Lin smiles at me with a sparkle in her eye, and I realize that she's not as tired as she said she was.

"You are insatiable," I tell her.

17

Lin and I lie in post coital bliss on her bed, our legs wrapped around each other's, my left arm around her shoulders and her head on my chest. The date is 1.73. We've been awake on the *Armstrong* for seventy-three days. It was day 29 or 30 when I showed that childbirth video to Lin. We've been sexually active, hyperactive is probably a better word for it, for 43 days. Can that be right? Lin's period arrived on day 31 or 32, so that's still over forty days without a trace of blood during our couplings. That's a long time.

"Hey," I say.

"Hey."

"It's been a long time since you had your period."

"My what?"

"Your period. When you had blood come out of your vagina." I have to remember that she's only ever had two periods since waking up in the pod.

"That's good."

"It means you may be pregnant."

"Pregnant?" Lin says in a dreamy voice, as if she's trying to recall that word.

"You may have a baby growing inside you."

Lin's body tenses. After a moment, she sits up and looks down at me.

"How you know?"

"I don't know for sure. We should have tests, but I don't know if they will still work."

"I want know."

She bursts off the bed and pulls on my arm to try to get me up. I sit up, yanking my arm away from her as I would fall onto my face on the floor if I let her keep pulling.

"I'm coming," I tell her when she tries to grab at me again.

The pregnancy tests are in a box in the medical supply section of the storage area. I have no idea if the chemicals in them will still work. They are three billion years old, but they spent all of those three billion years in a freezing zero-gravity vacuum. I pull one of them out of the box. Lin holds her hand out, expecting me to give it to her.

"You don't even know what to do with one of these."

Even as I say it, I realize that I don't know exactly how they work either. I take the box with me along with the test and walk to the nearest lavatory. I stand next to the commode reading the instructions as Lin seems to bounce on the balls of her feet. The first listing is to check the expiration date to make sure the test is still good. I almost laugh.

"Ok," I say and open the test stick. I pull a plastic cap off one end and hold it up for Lin. "You pee on this part of it."

Lin's face scrunches up in a look of disgust that I find endearing. I hand her the stick, and she straddles the commode holding the stick under her. With no self-consciousness, she crouches over the toilet. Once Lin gets a steady stream going, I take her hand and guide the end of the pregnancy test under that flow.

"That should be good," I say after a few seconds, taking the plastic stick from her.

I put the cap back on the now urine soaked end and set the whole thing on the edge of the sink. Lin sits down and finishes her business. By the time she has wiped and stands back up, the test is showing two lines instead of one. I look at the instructions on the box.

"Well, what do you know. It says positive."

"Positive means pregnant?"

"It does," I nod.

"Ha!" Lin's face brightens into the biggest grin I've ever seen her have. She bends over, hands on her abdomen. "I have a baby!"

"If we trust this three billion year old test."

Lin stands up and jumps out into the corridor. "Yea!" She acts like a kid, which in many ways, she is.

While Lin's reaction is one of joy, I feel a crushing weight of fear. What was I thinking? Jordan had his grand plans for this mission, but now it's just Lin and me out here, and Lin has a whole bunch of learning to do. She knows nothing about the mission or why we're here. And now we are adding a baby to that mix. I had been leaning toward moving down to the planet surface early just to ease my claustrophobia, but that is out of the question now. We will have to stay on the *Armstrong* for at least the two years now, and maybe more since we have provisions for it. Of course, we could get down to the planet, catch some microbe that makes us all sick and kills us before we ever get started, and then all my stressing about this would have been for nothing.

I walk out of the room and past the dancing Lin, lean against the wall, and take a deep breath. *It'll be all right,* I tell myself. *This is why we are here. This is the only reason we're here. To have lots and lots of babies and hope humanity takes hold.*

Even though I'm trying to separate myself from Earth Kevin's memories, I can't help but think back to the time Cynthia told me, Earth Kevin, that she was pregnant, those feelings of fear and responsibility and joy. Why don't I feel joy now? Part of me still feels married to Cynthia, so I've had those feelings of wrongness the last few weeks, like I'm cheating on her. Intellectually, I know that's silly. Cynthia has been gone for three billion years. But in my mind, I just saw her three months ago when she visited during the training for this crazy mission.

I leave Lin to her dancing celebration and start walking a fast lap around the wheel section, wishing I could be walking around my neighborhood in Box Elder. When Lin sees me, she runs to catch up.

"Laps again?"

"Walking helps me clear my head," I say.

"You sad?"

I shake my head. "No, not sad. Overwhelmed.

Scared."

"Why scared? Baby not hurt you."

"No, the baby won't hurt me. But I — we — will be responsible for the baby. We have to take care of it, feed it, change it, teach it. That's a lot."

Lin walks silently alongside me for a moment. "You good teacher. Take care of me. You take care of baby good too."

She takes my hand when that doesn't seem to lighten my mood. I slow my pace and look at her. Lin smiles, her eyes big and bright, and I feel a profound love for her, probably for the first time.

"Thank you for that," I say. "I try my best. But then again, I'm the only teacher you've ever had."

"You good teacher. Baby be fine."

"You'll be the baby's mommy."

Her eyes grow even bigger, and her smile turns into an expression of awe.

"Mommy, me?"

"Yes."

"How?"

"I'll teach you how to be a mommy," I say. "I'll be the baby's daddy, you know."

Lin's bottom lip quivers, and tears roll down her cheeks. "I no have mommy."

I sigh and take her in my arms.

"I know," I say softly into her ear. "I've tried to be everything, mommy, daddy, teacher, lover. You deserve more than me, but that's just not possible now."

Lin cries softly on my shoulder. Even though her mind was a blank because the memory download failed, the intelligence of Dr. Bascombe must have been encoded in her genes. She understands far more than I've given her credit for, and she is mourning what she never had.

"I'm sorry," I say in a soft voice. "This is not the way we should be. We are supposed to be born into loving families, raised by parents who love us. And you — we never got that."

I feel somewhat reluctant to include myself in that because I do have memories of growing up in a family. The parents weren't perfect, but I never doubted that they loved me. But the reality is that I am also a clone, and I don't want Lin to feel so alone in this situation.

"I love you," I tell her.

"Love you too."

18

The following morning, I am awakened by the sound of Lin throwing up in the lavatory next to our bed. I groan, roll out of bed, and rush to her side, holding her hair back as she spits out whatever is left in her mouth.

"Yuck," she says.

"Yep, you're definitely pregnant."

"I sick."

"It's called morning sickness. It's a symptom of pregnancy. Having a baby is not always wine and roses."

"What?"

"Nothing. Just an expression."

Lin gives me a questioning look as she rises from the commode and moves to the sink.

"Wine was an alcoholic drink made out of grapes.

Which we don't have on board. And roses were flowers. Also not on board. Forget I mentioned it."

Lin turns the water on and rinses her mouth before brushing her teeth. I remember seeing several boxes of pre-natal vitamins under the pregnancy tests. They are probably not any good, but that's what I thought about the pregnancy tests. Does removing heat, gravity, and atmosphere literally freeze things like these in time?

Lin and I shower as has become our routine. Once we have air dried and have brushed our hair, we start toward the galley.

"Do you feel like eating?" I ask her.

She nods and then stops for a couple of seconds, her mouth clamped shut, before running to the nearest lavatory again. I follow her and hold her hair again.

"Do you want to go lie down?" I ask as she rinses her mouth at the sink again.

She looks at my reflection in the mirror and nods. I walk her back to her bed and then go make breakfast. I make the normal amount for two, thinking I would just eat all of it if Lin doesn't want any food. I am feeling fairly hungry in spite of the smells and sounds of Lin's morning sickness.

Lin arrives just as I'm sitting down with a healthy plate of food.

"I hungry," she says, looking at my plate and then at the meager portion left next to the grill.

I'm not sure that she should be eating so soon after throwing up, but I slide my plate over to her and rise to retrieve what's left for myself. By the time I sit back down, she has scarfed down more than half of what was on the plate.

"I hope you can keep that down."

She looks up at me with a questioning look.

"I don't want you to throw up again."

"I feel fine," she says with a shrug.

"I hope so."

I watch Lin carefully as I eat, but she shows no sign of feeling bad. In fact, she looks at me after she swallows her last bite and says, "More?"

I still have two pieces of protein bacon and half of a cucumber left, so I slide my plate over to her without even thinking about how hungry I might be later. I could get up and make another breakfast, but I decide that if I get too hungry, we would just have lunch early.

"You feel better?" I ask her when she finishes.

She smiles and nods. I remember something my grandmother used to say to the pregnant women in the family at the dinner table, "You're eating for two now," but I don't repeat it. The thought of her saddens me, both because she's only a memory now and because she wasn't my grandmother. She was Earth Kevin's grandmother. Then I think about how she would feel about me disclaiming her, and I am even more saddened.

"I eat your food?" Lin says, a look of concern on her face.

I snap myself out of my reverie and shake my head. "It's fine."

"Make more?"

"Do you want more?"

Lin shrugs.

"I can wait."

"K," she says.

After we have cleaned up from breakfast, I go to the control room console. Lin follows and sits beside me. She has taken an active interest in the planet surface since I told her that we would be living there after the baby comes. I didn't tell her how long after the baby comes though. It might be another year. There might even be a second baby by the time we leave.

We are above the site of Lander 7 with its working drone, rapidly approaching a terminator from day to night. I switch over to it, and the image from the drone camera fills the big screen. It is still docked onto the lander, the camera facing out toward the west and the setting sun. I haven't yet done much night surveillance, so I don't know what nocturnal creatures may be about.

"Pretty," Lin says, talking about the orange and red light reflecting from the scattered clouds on the horizon.

"Yeah," I say. "Sunsets are beautiful. We got some amazing ones in Texas. And in South Dakota."

"Sunset?"

"Yeah, when the day ends, the sun sets, and night starts. We see the planet turn away from the sun up here, but when we're down there on the surface, it looks like the sun is moving across the sky. And when it disappears over the horizon, we call it a sunset. Then it's night, and when the sun comes back for the next day, we call that a sunrise."

"I want go," Lin says, pointing at the screen.

"We will."

"Now?"

"No, not now. It's a one way trip. Once we go, we can never come back here."

"I want go."

I sigh. "Life will get a whole lot more difficult once we are down there. We'll have to spend most of our time finding food. We won't have the TV. No more *Bluey* or *Sesame Street*." That's not entirely true as there will be video monitors on the transport craft, and I plan on copying the library from the main hard drive here to one of the ones on the transports. But I anticipate being so busy with living that we won't have much time to watch anything.

Lin looks back toward the lounge. "Oh."

"Yeah."

Movement on the screen draws my attention. A creature on two legs is stepping toward the probe.

"What the hell?" I say.

The creature looks almost human, with two legs and arms in proportion with the rest of its body. Like most of the animals I'd seen on the planet, it is hairless, with reddish brown skin that matches the color of the rocks I'd seen among the foliage. It has male genitalia and carries a rod or staff in his right hand. Behind him walks another just like him except that this one is obviously female, with what would be medium sized breasts on a human.

"Who that?" Lin says.

"I don't know."

The two beings creep toward the lander which has been sitting there for about twenty years. But it's probably making noise now since I have activated the drone and its camera. The male reaches out with the stick and with the end of it appears to touch the side of the craft, next to the drone's bay.

"Shit," I say, thinking that I don't want to wait for him

to damage the drone. I also don't want him to see the drone flying around, but I don't think I have any choice.

I send the drone out of its bay and straight up about twenty feet. When I turn it around to see the ground, the male and female humanoids are running back to the woods. I fly the drone above them, curious about where they would go and whether they would get there while I could still see them in the diminishing light. They follow a trail through the trees. I am barely able to follow them through the few breaks in the foliage. When the trail emerges at the foot of a small mountain, the two break off and disappear into a cave.

I try to turn the drone's light on to see into the cave, but it doesn't work. The sun has set completely now, so I quickly fly the drone back to the lander before it gets too dark to see. The *Armstrong* passes out of range of the Lander 7 soon after I get the drone docked. I sit staring at the blank screen for what seems like several minutes. In all the video footage I have watched, not just from Lander 7 but from all of them, I have never seen anything remotely resembling humanoids. I turn my head and see Lin watching me silently. I give her what is probably an uneasy smile.

"They afraid," she says.

"Yes, they were."

"Afraid of us?"

"Of the flying drone, yes. They haven't even seen us yet."

I can't help but think of those camouflaged flying bat things. Are those the apex predators of this planet, forcing other species underground and making them virtually nocturnal?

I play the video back and freeze the screen with both of the creatures in the shot. I zoom in on their faces which have two eyes and an opening under them where a mouth would go on a human face. Neither of them appears to have noses, so I zoom in even further on the male and see two small openings just above the mouth.

"Humanoid," I say.

"They look strange," Lin says.

"They're from another planet from us."

Still zoomed in, I lower the view to the rod in the male's hand. It is smooth and curved with what appears to be a padded grip where he holds it. And it looks to have been painted purple. Is it a manufactured cane? If they are capable of making tools like this, they are smarter than the animals on this planet. It makes me wonder what they have underground. Is there an entire civilization down there? And, morally, should Lin and I be invading their planet like we are planning?

Of course, it's too late to think about that. We are here, and we either go down to the surface or die up here in space.

19

I wake up early the next day and sit at the console, waiting for the *Armstrong* to come around the planet enough to be in range of Lander 7 again. As soon it connects, I activate the camera and feel relieved when it still works. The humanoids could have come back out and attacked it after seeing the drone flying. It is just sitting there, after all. I fire up the drone's propellors and send it toward the cave entrance I'd seen the night before. When it enters, I see, with the help of the drone's light, a smooth floor with stairs cut into the rock. A soft glow seems to come from the depths.

It never occurs to me that I would lose signal with the drone underground until the video screen suddenly goes dark.

"Shit."

Luckily, the drones all have a failsafe command to return to the lander dock whenever communication is lost with the *Armstrong*. The video feed returns as the drone exits the cave into the bright sunlight. I take control of the drone's flight again and steer it around the hill with the cave entrance. At this point, I don't know what I'm looking for. What I really want to see is underground where I can't get to. I see something several hundred yards from the cave entrance, plants in a series of straight rows, fruits and vegetables of various shapes and colors hanging from them or just sitting on the ground. As the drone keeps turning around the hill, the full size and scope of the farm comes into view, covering acres and acres. How did I miss this?

"Because from the air, the plants all merge and just look like part of the jungle," I say out loud.

I needed to see it from this lower vantage point. I fly the drone between rows, noting some plants that look like corn, some that are similar to squash or beans, and others that look like nothing I have ever seen before.

As my countdown to orbital signal loss nears zero, I fly the drone back toward the lander. The video feed ends about halfway back, but I know that the drone will continue on to its docking station. I click on the newly created video file, and watch it three times, concentrating on the cave and freezing it at various points. The stairs appear smooth and new, but they do look to have been cut directly out of the stone, not manufactured from other material and then installed. There don't appear to be any signs or labels in the entrance to the cave, nothing that might say, "City this way," or "Watch your step," or anything like that.

The footage of the garden interests me the most, although it's too big to be called a simple garden. This is a full-fledged farm, with each row being at least three hundred yards long. I open a notepad and start cataloging the plants that are visible. My biggest question is, how many of those humanoids does this farm support? I don't know the harvest schedule for any of these plants. The temperature rarely, if ever, gets below seventy degrees Fahrenheit, so the growing season could be perpetual.

The big question on my mind is, how advanced is the civilization of these creatures? The two I saw on the video were naked, but that doesn't tell me anything. If they were coming out to garden, that may just be standard operating procedure on a planet as warm as this one. And when Lin and I show up on the surface, we'll be naked, and I consider us to be fairly advanced. We did come over a million light years to get here.

I had been leaning heavily toward making the site of Lander 7 the spot where we land when we leave the *Armstrong*, but I may have to reconsider that. Whatever challenges Lin and I will face on this planet, we don't want to also be outnumbered right next to a civilization that may or may not be hostile toward us. But that begs the question, how pervasive is this humanoid civilization across the entire planet? Are they only in this region or this continent, or are they worldwide? I'll have to go back through the video footage from the other landers and look for signs of other entrances to an underground civilization or any farming on the surface.

Before I can click the notepad icon to start typing my to-do list, Lin pulls my chair away from the keyboard and sits on my lap facing me.

"Morning," she says.

"Good morning Lin."

She has a playful glint in her eye as she softly bites over part of her lower lip. And she knows I find that look irresistible.

"What you doing?"

"Same as usual. Trying to figure out how it's going to be when we get down to the planet surface."

"When we go?"

"A long time. After the baby comes. Maybe even longer."

Lin sighs and looks around at the interior of the *Armstrong*.

"Want somewhere new."

"Don't be in such a rush. Like I said, when we leave here, we can never come back. And like I already told you, there's no TV down there. No *Bluey* or *Sesame Street*."

Lin looks down at my expanding penis, takes it in her hand and bites her lower lip again.

"OK," I say and pick her up and take her back to our bed.

Lin and I lie together in a post-coital embrace as I catch my breath. I apparently doze off, because the next thing I know, she's shaking me awake.

"Kev!"

I look at her and see the fear in her face.

"What's wrong?"

She holds her hand up. There's a small amount of blood on two of her fingers.

"What's that from?"

She points down to her vagina.

"Shit," I say and spring up out of bed.

I look at my own genitals, but I don't see any blood there. So the bleeding just started after sex, not during.

"Let me see," I say.

She lies back, and I spread her legs open. I am relieved to find very little blood, either on her or on the mattress.

"It's just a little spotting," I say.

"Spotting?"

"It's normal. It happened with Cynthia during two of her pregnancies."

"Cynthia? Who that?"

I automatically begin to say that she's my wife, but I stop myself. I know I must have talked about Earth Kevin's life to her before she was able to understand and before we became sexual partners. But I don't think I've mentioned Cynthia since Lin has been able to understand things. Hell, I've been trying not to think about what is forever gone. I decide to ignore the question.

"Do you feel bad?"

She shrugs.

I shrug back at her. "What does that mean?"

"I fine," she says.

"We can go check you on the ultrasound. We need to do that anyway."

"Who Cynthia?"

"She was Earth Kevin's wife."

"Earth Kevin?"

Lin sits up and looks at me with those large questioning

eyes. I give her a serious look for a moment before I answer.

"Earth Kevin is the original of me."

"What?" Lin says, not understanding.

"You and I are clones. We are copies of people who lived on Earth a long, long time ago."

Lin continues to look at me.

"Earth is where the shows you watch came from. *Sesame Street* was supposed to be a street in New York. On Earth."

"Copies? We not real?"

"Yes, we're real, but we are clones. We are just like certain people who lived on Earth."

An idea occurs to me, and I take her hand and pull her to her feet. "Here."

She follows me to the lounge and with voice commands, I tell Alexis to bring up a list of our mission training videos. I select the first one on the list, and we sit down on the floor to watch.

The video starts in Jordan's conference room. All six of us are sitting around the table. The camera is mounted high above the end of the long table. I remember the little bubble in the ceiling in that spot of the room. Jordan sat at the head of the table. Linda and I were on one side, to Jordan's left, and Stacey, Lilly, and Kacey were on the other side. All six of us were looking toward the camera, at the screen that Lin and I can't see because it was directly below that camera.

"This is the *Armstrong* as it will spend most of its existence," Jordan says on the screen, "hurtling through interstellar space. It has no crew and no power. We are using the cold of space to keep the embryos frozen. As I told most of you, there will be six *Armstrongs*, each with a programmed destination. These destinations are based on what little we know of those identified planets outside our solar system and constitute the ones most likely to be able to sustain life as we know it. Of course, what is known is theoretical and could be entirely wrong. Once the *Armstrong* enters a star system, it will power up using energy from the star, and the AI will take over. If the AI determines that no planets in the system would sustain human life, it will send the *Armstrong* on its way, using a combination of an engine burn and a gravity assist from the system's star."

"Who that?" Lin asks.

"Alexis, pause," I say, and the video freezes. "That is Jordan Walker. But that's not what I want to show you." I jump up and step over to the view screen and point at Linda and me, Earth Kevin. "See these two people?"

Lin nods.

"That's us. Or the original us's. We are clones of them. Copies, like I told you."

Lin continues to look at the screen, a perplexed look on her face.

"They are much older than we are now. Earth Kevin was 48 and Earth Linda was sixty-something there. But we are both about 18 or 19 now."

I restart the video so that Lin can see and hear Earth Linda talk, but Jordan is in full lecture mode. He goes on about what the ship's AI would do once it got to a star system with a planet capable of supporting human life, how the ship would enter orbit, start spinning the wheel section to simulate gravity before the cloning process begins.

"Those bodies cannot live in zero-g and then expect to be able to handle the gravity of a planet," Jordan says. "So we have to simulate gravity in orbit. Unfortunately, to get from the wheel to the service module, we'll either have to turn off the gravity spin or perform an EVA, a spacewalk."

"Why would we ever need to get to the service module?" Earth Kevin asks on the screen.

Lin laughs and glances at me and then back at the screen.

"We shouldn't until we are ready to go down to the planet," Jordan answers. "The transport vessels are stored in and will launch from the service module."

The six of them watch the screen for several seconds, giving the illusion that they are watching Lin and me, before Earth Linda says, "There are three landers?"

Lin gasps, realizing, I guess, that the voice sounds like hers.

"Yes," Jordan answers.

"Why are there three of them?"

"Redundancy. If something, God forbid, were to happen to one, we don't want all six of us dying."

"But they'll all land in the same place?" Lilly asks.

"That's the plan. We intend to be a community. Those little probes you saw leave the ship in the animation are probes sent to different locations on the planet's surface. They will monitor weather and the flora and fauna of the area over the twenty or so years while we are growing and developing on the *Armstrong*. We should then be able to make an informed decision as to what the best location for our community will be."

Jordan pauses and looks at the five people around the

table. "Any questions?"

"Oh my God, yes!" Earth Linda says, and the five around the table all burst into laughter. Lin laughs along with them, seemingly enchanted by her older self.

20

I stop the video there and take Lin to the infirmary where there are a couple of ultrasound devices. She is quiet while I get her into position. She hasn't learned any body shame, having never worn clothes in her life, so the only awkwardness comes from my pauses as I try to remember the all too brief training on the equipment we took while preparing for this mission. It takes a few minutes, but I find the baby on the screen, its heartbeat strong and fast.

"See, the baby is fine," I tell her.

Lin smiles, but her eyes seem vacant.

"You okay?"

Lin shrugs. "I not smart."

"Yes, you are."

"No. Not like old Linda. Not like you."

I sigh as I clean and put away the ultrasound wand.

"You were supposed to have old Linda's memories, the same way I have old Kevin's. But something went wrong, and your memory download didn't work."

"Why?"

"I don't know. Maybe the files got corrupted. Maybe something was wrong with the upload back on Earth. I don't know."

"You want me like old Linda, so we can talk."

I look at Lin, thinking about the weeks we'd already spent together, all the things she has learned along the way, and I shake my head. "No, I don't want that. You're perfect just the way you are. And I don't know what's worse, having all these memories of Earth and friends and family, knowing that I'll never ever see any of it, any of them, again. Or not having the memories at all but knowing that there was an Earth that you've come from. It seems bad either way."

Lin must see the pain in my face as she sits up and pulls me into a hug.

"We are so utterly alone, you and me," I say. "All we have is each other."

We hold each other for a long moment before I step away and finish with the ultrasound equipment.

"You have Cynthia on TV?" Lin asks.

I had given Jordan access to my family videos in the Cloud for him to include in the *Armstrong's* library, but I haven't had the strength to look to see if they are there. Can I stand to see images of my wife and children knowing that they are now reduced to atoms by time? As much as I try to convince myself that Earth Kevin is a separate entity, the memories that I have in my head still seem real and fresh. I can't help but think of them as *my* family.

"I think so," I reply.

"Can I see?"

I sigh, and Lin gives me a pleading look. I smile back at her.

"Some things are universal to the human condition," I say. "Every woman I've ever known wants to know who her man's ex's were."

"What?"

"Nothing."

I hold my hand out to her. She takes it, and I help her off the examining table. We walk back to the lounge, and I query Alexis for a list of folders. There is one for each of the crew members, and I feel a stab of sadness that the other four aren't with us. Then I wonder if I should be sad that they have been spared this.

"Alexis, open the Kevin folder."

My folder opens to a long list of video files. I see baseball games I played as a kid back in the 2020's, my wedding to Cynthia, the birth of all three kids, vacation videos, and many more. I didn't want to watch the wedding, so I select video of our first vacation to South Dakota, the one that made us fall in love with the place enough to move there several years later.

The first shot is of Cynthia and me in front of Mount Rushmore. We are standing near the information booth, all the different flags of the states flying along the path behind us, and we are looking back at the kids, one of whom is holding the camera.

"So what do you all think?" Cynthia asks them.

I am around forty years old here. Lin leans forward,

looking at me with my arm around Cynthia.

"You?"

"Yes, that's me. Kevin."

"'That Cynthia?"

"Yes."

My mouth is dry as I look at the images on the screen. Kaitlyn and Bobby run up and stand in front of us, looking back at Thomas with the camera, and perform a little dance. They are so young. Kaitlyn is only eight, and Bobby is five and won't start Kindergarten until the end of that summer. The longing to see them again is like a weight on my chest. I laugh at their high pitched voices even as the tears flow down my cheeks. The video stops, and then Thomas has replaced me in the shot. I'm now holding the camera, and I see my entire family posing in front of the four Presidents. Thomas, my firstborn, is only ten here. And they are all impossibly gone, all four of them. Three billion years and one million light years separate us. How the hell am I still here, breathing manufactured oxygen so far away from anything and everything I've ever known?

I can't watch anymore. I get up, a sob escaping my throat, and rush back to my space, the pod in which I awoke in this clone body. At some point over three billion years ago, the original me woke up after the memory upload, got a ride to SFO, and flew home to Rapid City. He took Cynthia in his arms and kissed her, hugged Kaitlyn and Bobby, and lived the rest of his days, watching his kids grow up and lead lives of their own. Perhaps they married and had kids of their own. Grandkids that I will never meet. This isn't fair that I'm not the one who got to go home, and I can only feel nothing but envy and hate for that original me, for not ever even considering what I, his clone, would be going through. Of course, he could never comprehend the time and distance between him and this iteration of the *Armstrong*. Hell, I'm here, and even I don't comprehend it.

Almost blind from the raging tears in my eyes, I collapse onto my plastic covered mattress and bury my face in my arms. Now that the first sob has escaped, I can't help but cry like a child, something I haven't done since I was a teenager.

"Kev?"

Lin touches my back between my shoulder blades.

"What?" I manage to say.

"Sorry."

"It's OK. Go watch the video. Go see what life on Earth was like. I can't watch it anymore."

I keep my face buried, but I feel Lin leave. The sobbing has stopped, but I continue lying there trying to forget everything until sleep takes me.

21

I decide to keep looking forward rather than back, and I throw myself into my work, researching landing sites, growing and cooking our food, weekly check-ups on Lin and the baby, diagnostics on the *Armstrong*, and whatever else I can think of to do. So far, I have not found any evidence of agriculture or those humanoid creatures at any of the other landing probe sites beyond that of Lander 7. Speaking of Lander 7, I make use of every available daylight opportunity to fly the drone around the location looking for other signs of the humanoids' level of civilization. I've also been hoping for another glimpse of the humanoids themselves, but so far, I only get an opportunity over that site at dusk or dawn about once a week. Blasting lights during full night doesn't sound like a good idea to me, so I have refrained from it for now. I've never seen them in full daylight, so they must come out to work the fields at night. If they live underground, they are probably able to see at night and might be blinded by full sunlight.

The humanoids still haven't done anything to damage or disable Lander 7 or its drone which surprises me. If they are anything like we humans, they have to be curious even if they are afraid. Then again, if those camouflaged flying bat things are the apex predators of this planet, maybe the humanoids are averse to anything that can fly. Scaring them is another reason for not flying the drone at night, but I'm about to give that up and do it anyway. I need to know how advanced these creatures are.

Lin has immersed herself in the videos from Earth, watching one after the other from everybody's folders, including the other four crew members whose clones did not live to see this iteration of the *Armstrong*. I think seeing other humans interact with each other is good for her. And Earth Linda's folder includes quite a few videos from her younger years when she looked much more like Lin than the older lady in that video we had watched of our mission training meeting.

Lin and I didn't have sex for an entire week after the spotting incident. Since it happened right after intercourse, I can only imagine that Lin connected the two and therefore left me alone. On the eighth day, I walked over to where she was watching more of the mission training videos, the six of us on screen in full astronaut gear under water simulating a spacewalk, and started massaging her shoulders. We both took it slow and had a very satisfying session with zero blood. After that, Lin's sex drive seems to have returned. She still spends all her TV time watching crew members' videos.

I had set an alert reminding me to connect to Lander 7, and it pops up on the screen even as I am already connecting to Lander 7. I dismiss it, proud of myself for remembering before it had appeared. It is well into night in the area when the image from the drone's camera appears on the big screen. A few random clicking noises come through via the audio feed, and I turn the volume up. There is a rhythmic beat underlying the clicking. Is that music? I disengage the drone from the lander and have to turn the volume back down because of the noise of the drone's engines right next to the microphone. I keep the lights off and fly it in the direction of the fields I had seen earlier. I'm afraid to fly low and hit something, so I stay high. The music, if that's what it is, seems louder, but with the drone engines almost overpowering everything, it's difficult to tell. It's too dark to see exactly where I am, but it seems like I should be directly over the fields. I switch the light on with the camera pointed down and look to see dozens of humanoids dropping their tools and scattering away from the drone's path. I feel bad for frightening them like I have, but I can see what appear to be hoes and rakes that they have been using on the fields.

I fly the drone down low and look at each tool. The music stops as I am examining the hoe. The head appears to be made of some kind of metal and is attached to what looks like a wooden pole. It looks like it could have been purchased at The Home Depot on Earth. I hear cries and the sound of footsteps in the dirt, running. I have started a stampede. I fly up again, wanting a better look at these creatures. I fly with the lights on, and I see a line of them running toward the cave entrance, all of them on two legs with arms pumping like a human sprinting in a race.

I am the invader, I and my flying drone. I am everything we humans feared during the UFO scares back on Earth.

"Sorry," I say even as I fly the drone to within a few yards of them.

Many of them glance back, their eyes and mouths big and round in what I can only imagine is an expression of terror. I will replay this footage back over and over, but for now, I need to capture as much as I can and worry about noting anything special or distinctive for later. The drone flies past and hovers over the cave entrance, catching all the running humanoids as they enter, ducking low as they do, some of them even crawling to stay as far from the drone as possible. Once the area around the entrance is clear of them, I fly back toward the fields, capturing on video any items that may have been dropped or left behind. Among the gardening tools, there are what appear to be over-the-shoulder pouches or purses, paper wrappers, and even what looks like it might be a book. I bring the drone down to the book thing. I turn the drone slowly so that the camera pans over the cover which is a plain brown with unknown white characters on it. I wish I could open it, but the drone is not equipped with arms. I check my clock to see how long I'll still have connectivity even as the image on the screen fades.

"Damn it," I say.

The *Armstrong's* orbit has moved me out of range. I back the video up to look at the book. That's the only thing it can be. It's thin, but I can make out the striations of the pages on the sides. The cover appears to be paper, like a trade paperback book back on Earth. They have language. They have tools. They have a civilization.

Lin and I are intruders. We don't belong here. I think back to our history, how European invaders took over North America and killed or subjugated the native populations. That sort of thing happened throughout our history. Is that what we are? Is that what the human species is? Did Jordan even consider this when he developed this mission?

I push away from the console, stand up, and take a walk around the wheel. As I pass the lounge, I see that Lin is watching one of Linda Bascombe's classroom lectures. On the screen, she looks like she's in her late thirties which was about the time I took her classes as an undergraduate. I wonder if I, or Earth Kevin, was in the room during this particular lecture. But I don't stop walking. If Lin sees me, she doesn't say anything.

I can't help but wish that Dr. Bascombe were here to offer her insight and wisdom. But if the memory download had worked on Lin, she wouldn't be the Lin that's here now, the Lin I have grown to love. Is it possible to want two opposing things? Earth Linda would have been able to offer valuable insight just like she did during training.

Whatever I do now, I can't select the site of Lander 7 as our future home. I'm not here as an ambassador to establish relations with another species; I am here to forge a new home for humanity. Taking some other species's home away from them in order to do that is not something I am willing to do. But I'm also not willing to just remain here in orbit until we die. I can only hope that these humanoids' reach doesn't extend to any of the other continents.

22

The next time the *Armstrong's* orbit brings me in range of Lander 7, neither the probe nor the drone is responsive. I can only assume that the humanoid Edenites mounted some kind of attack and disabled them.

"Good for you," I say even though I feel like I should be angry at the destruction of property and the inability to see that site.

The disabling of the drone is the first sign of aggression displayed by the Edenites which further validates my decision to rule the site out of any future settlement. In twenty years, Lander 7 has been the only one of the forty probes sent to the surface that relayed any evidence of an intelligent sentient species on the planet. It would be stupid to then select that as the site for our settlement.

That would be like looking for a fight.

There is another site on the southern continent, far away from the Edenites, that showed promise as a site for settlement. Lander 15 is there, but it hasn't responded for a few years. Still, the climate readings from the first dozen or so years and the saved videos of the area look good, with lots of game for hunting and fertile ground for farming. And it's far enough away from the coast that it's not subject to the tidal floods brought by the occasional alignment of Eden's three moons.

If I'm serious about that site as a possible home, I can send one of the three large landing craft to the site. The three transport ships are designed to connect together once on the surface to create spacious living quarters for us. Lin and I will only really need one of those ships since our other four crew members didn't survive. I could remote pilot one of them down to that spot and use the tools on it to get new readings and images. I need to do a test run to the surface with one of those ships anyway. Each ship has a heat shield for entry into the atmosphere. Once the velocity has slowed down enough, that heat shield is jettisoned enabling the rocket engines underneath to further slow the descent. A large parachute should also deploy to ensure a soft landing.

With the disintegration of our clothing on the *Armstrong*, I have concerns about those parachutes. They should be packed in the ships with enough compression that the zero gravity shouldn't have affected the material. I'm assuming, of course, that my theory about our clothing unraveling because of the three billion years in zero g is correct.

I pull up the folder for Lander 15 and start watching the

videos again, this time looking for any indication of any civilization. It is dull and tedious, and I am almost asleep when the camouflage green catlike creature I've seen before saunters across the screen. I stop the video and check the clock. It's almost time to eat, so I stand up and head to the kitchen.

Lin is already there, slicing a zucchini. Two 3-D printed steaks sizzle on the grill.

"Hello Kevin," she says.

Her speech patterns are becoming more like Earth Linda's the more she watches videos from the library.

"It's Kev," I say again.

Lin is quiet as she slides the zucchini slices into a saucepan.

"Do you find it odd?" Lin says and then stops.

"Find what odd?"

She is trying to come up with the correct wording. "That you want to be far from your old self, and I want to be close to mine?"

Still wondering which of us got the worse deal regarding our old memories, I start to say no, that I don't find it odd, but I stop myself.

"Yes," I finally answer. "I do find it odd. Everything about this whole situation is odd. We are, probably, the only two human beings left in the universe, and even if we aren't, the others are so far away that we might as well be the only ones. So yeah, I find it odd. I find it odd that we are so far away from Earth that we can't even comprehend it."

Lin turns the steaks over as I take a spatula and stir the zucchini.

"You sound mad," she says.

"Yeah, I kind of am. My old self went into this thing without even thinking about what it would be like for us."

"You remember doing it? 'Going into this thing'?"

"Yeah."

"So it was you who did it then. Right?"

I drop the spatula on the counter and sit at the table.

Lin looks at me. "You hate him. You hate yourself."

I gaze back at her and shrug.

"Stop hating yourself," she says. "It doesn't do any good."

Lin stands there, naked and pregnant, her hands on her hips, but I can't help but be reminded of Dr. Bascombe in lecture mode in a business suit.

"You sound just like her," I say, realizing how tense I have been even as I try to relax.

"I wish I could remember."

"And I wish I can't remember. You were so much smarter than me, much more philosophical. You probably would have been able to make sense of these issues where I can't."

Lin shrugs. She serves both our plates as I continue sitting at the table, wondering how Lin could have absorbed so much wisdom from watching those old videos.

"I remember what we've lost, and you don't," I tell her. "I kept thinking I got the worst of this, knowing that I can never regain any of what I miss about my old life."

"Instead of thinking about what you lost, think about what you have to gain. We have an entire world all to ourselves."

"Well, not all to ourselves." I tell her about the Edenites and how I frightened them to the point that they disabled the drone and the lander.

"The drone didn't hurt any of them?" Lin asks.

"No. Not unless they hurt themselves in the stampede to get away from it."

"They destroyed the drone?"

"I can't connect to it, so they disabled it in some way."

"Because they were afraid of it?"

"Yes."

"So we're not going to land there because we're afraid of them. That they'll do to us what they did to the drone?"

"No, that's not why. I don't want us to have to hurt them."

"Because they would be afraid of us?"

"Yes."

Lin sits and thinks about this a few minutes as we finish eating. I can almost see the wheels turning.

"Is that how wars start? People being afraid of each other and one of them doing something before the other one can do something else?"

"That's how some of them started, I'm sure."

She takes both plates and utensils to the sink and starts washing them.

"That's silly."

"That's human nature," I say.

"But we are the only humans left, right? That's what you keep saying."

"Yes."

"So we change human nature. We raise our kids to be different. And they raise their kids to be different, and on and on."

"I hope so."

23

I spend another few weeks looking at video recordings and live video from other probes before settling on the site of Lander 15 for a test landing. That site had already been in my top two, along with Lander 7 before I crossed that off the list, so it only makes sense that 15 is left at the top. But I still want to be sure. We only have three transport craft, only two of which could be used for test landings. The third would have to take Lin and me down to the surface. Once I've gone through the weather history and all the video at least a dozen times, I start making plans to remote pilot the transport craft to that spot.

The transport ships launch from the center cylinder section of the *Armstrong*. To get there, I will have to stop the gravity rotation of the wheel section. The axis of the wheel section is basically a sleeve that fits around the cylinder section, turning around it. When I stop the rotation, the hatches should line up and then connect automatically. Throughout this mission, the cylinder has been airless, so we'll also have to spend time floating around in zero-g while it pressurizes.

I remember very well the aftermath of my zero gravity experiment, the wet floors in all the lavatories and the little things that began floating when the gravity spin stopped and that crashed to the floor when I turned that spin back on. This time, I follow the proper procedure. Lin and I spend the morning going around the wheel section making sure the lids on the commodes are clamped shut and that everything is put in its proper place. We end those tasks back at the control console. I go down the checklist, making sure that we did everything.

"You ready?" I ask Lin.

She barely remembers the time I'd turned off the gravity back when I was doubting the reality of our situation, and she is excited about the idea of floating around.

"Yes," she replies.

"Alexis, turn off the gravity."

"Turning off gravity," the voice replies.

Lin and I sit at the console and wait for the rotation to slow and then stop. It's strange how we don't feel the wheel slowing. The view screen shows the planet, but that's from a camera on the cylinder section. I punch a few keys on the keyboard, and the current rotation speed of the wheel section is overlaid on the screen. We watch the numbers tick down until we feel our backsides lifting away from our chairs.

"This is fun," Lin says as she pushes off toward what

had been the ceiling and bumping her head.

"Careful."

I grab her on the rebound and look her in the eyes. She's trying to fight back tears.

"That hurt, didn't it?"

She frowns and nods. I pull her into a hug, gently caressing her head as we drift toward the lounge. A glance back at the big screen in the control room shows me that the doors have lined up and connected and that the cylinder section has another 83 minutes until full pressurization.

"We have an hour and a half to kill," I say. "What do you want to do?"

Her frown turns into a grin, and I know what she's thinking.

"Of course," I say. "Nothing like zero gravity to enhance the sexual experience."

Feeling like I may have strained a hamstring or two during our recreational activities, I float through the tunnel toward the cylinder section of the ship. Lin is right behind me. There is a ladder in the tunnel, one of the spokes on the big wheel, so that we could make this trip with the gravity spin enabled. Why we would want to make this trip with that spin enabled is still a mystery to me. We can't get into the cylinder while the wheel section is spinning. But the steps of the ladder make good handholds for pushing ourselves toward our destination.

The gauges that display the air pressure level in the airlock between the cylinder section and the wheel section look good, so I proceed. The lever that opens the hatch stubbornly stays in place when I try to pull it. What the hell would we do if we can't get it open? There is a space suit of unknown integrity for extra-vehicular activities. What if we get outside the *Armstrong*, and it leaks? Or, what if the suit is OK, but the airlock to the cylinder section is for some reason inaccessible? We'd never be able to get to the landing craft to get down to the planet. We'd either die on a space walk or live the rest of our days in orbit.

I see the metal pipe mounted on the wall next to the hatch and recall it is to be used as a lever for the hatch. Giving Lin a quick smile, I unhook the pipe and put one end in the hatch lever. I have to put my feet on the wall just below the pipe's mounting brackets to get resistance since there is no gravity. As I strain to turn the lever, I think to myself that this would make a good painting, *Male Nude Opens Hatch.* If only there were any artists alive to paint it. Using both leg and arm strength, the hatch lever slowly budges and loosens. Once it makes a half turn, I take my feet off the wall, mount the pipe back where it had been, and easily turn the lever with my hands.

I pull that hatch open to find another hatch, with a gap of about eighteen inches between the two. This one opens without any difficulty, and Lin and I float into a large open space.

"Oooh," Lin coos as she looks up and around, and I realize she has no memory or knowledge of anything outside that circular tube in which we live.

"Different, huh?"

"Yeah."

"Just wait until we get down to the planet. Wide open spaces, sky. You can't imagine."

When we reach the opposite wall, I grab the handle and pivot toward the first launch bay. *Human Transport One* sits inside just where I expect to find it. It is large and round with a sloped roof, as it is intended to serve as the first living quarters on the planet surface. The bottom of it is a big round disc that will serve as the heat shield for entering the planet's atmosphere.

I open the door and float into the cockpit. Lin follows behind and takes the seat next to me. We strap ourselves in just so we won't float up, and I power up the ship's console. All the diagnostics come back in normal ranges. The one I'm most concerned about, the integrity of the cloth of the parachute, isn't measured, but the pressurized container for that chute reads as normal. I set the controls to auto pilot and leave the console powered on. I move the weapons, two rifles and two handguns, along with the boxes of ammunition, from the transport ship to a closet just outside the launch bay. I'll put them into whatever transport ship Lin and I take to the surface, just in case this site doesn't work out.

"All right," I say to Lin, taking her hand. "Let's go to the cylinder control room and see how this thing does."

24

The control room in the cylinder section is a mirror image of the one in the wheel, although in a much more open space. The view screen isn't a screen but an actual window looking out at the planet. A small part of the wheel section, where we have been living these past few months, is visible at the edge of the window. Lin and I buckle the plastic-coated seatbelts so we won't have to fight floating away, and I power on the console. Once I'm connected to *Human Transport One*, I verify that the cabin pressurized after we left it. When I lock in the coordinates for the landing, the computer gives me a countdown of almost an hour and a half. That's when the *Armstrong* will be in optimum position above the planet to launch and land at that spot.

"I guess we wait again," I say to Lin.

She smiles and puts her hand on my thigh, batting her eyelashes at me.

"You overestimate my prowess and stamina," I say.

She laughs and spins her chair all the way around, unbuckles her seatbelt, and floats above me.

"Why we not float all the time?" Lin asks.

"Because we need to be acclimated to the planet if we are going to live there."

"We won't float on the planet?"

"Nope."

"Then I want us to stay here. And we can float."

"That's not an option. I'm already going stir crazy. And believe me, you'll get tired of floating soon. Especially when you have to go pee."

"The pee floats?"

"Everything floats."

Lin sighs and says, "Now I need to pee."

"Of course you do."

The cylinder section has several zero gravity restrooms as this part of the ship was designed to always be in zero-g. I help Lin use the funnel, activate the vacuum, and tell her to go ahead. She laughs at the suction on her vulva so much that I wonder if she might be getting sexually stimulated from it. And then I realize that Lin seems to get sexually stimulated by anything and everything. Of course, that thought makes me aroused which is always difficult to hide in our state of perpetual nudity. I decide to leave her to her business and float back to the control room.

I strap myself into the chair and watch the count down while Lin floats around in the large open spaces. I can't blame her for that. Her only memories are of being in a small circular tube. This cylinder section must look like the inside of The Superdome to her. I can't wait to get her outside once we leave the *Armstrong* and land on the planet.

Lin kicks off from one wall and turns in the air as if doing somersaults. Her abdomen is really big now with the baby's due date just a couple of months away. I read through the report of the *Transport One's* diagnostics, looking for any points of concern, but I don't spot any. Kacey Thomas, the pilot of our crew, could have given this the review it really needs, but her clone hadn't survived. I turn and watch Lin, the expression on her face like that of a child at Disneyland, and the massive weight of responsibility hits me. I have to be everything on this mission, commander, pilot, doctor, nurse, midwife, cook, teacher, mechanic, and janitor. I can't even blame Lin. It isn't her fault that her memory download failed. At least her body survived to adulthood. If she hadn't, then the mission would be pointless with no way to reproduce, my presence here just a waste of time.

If not for Lin, I would have already been on the planet. My stir craziness would have been compounded by loneliness, and I would have said fuck it and just taken one of the transport ships to the surface. And if I died in the attempt, nothing would have been lost. And if I had survived, I would have just lived out the rest of my days. There would be no use compiling data on this new planet if no one would ever see said data.

Thankfully, Lin is here, and she is learning at a rapid pace. As I watch her cavorting in the control room, I catch glimpses of the baby's shape pushing against her belly.

The baby is, of course, floating in his or her own zero gravity container. I wonder if the lack of gravity in the ship is affecting the baby in any way. I hope it's not, but we aren't going to be in zero-g very long. It also occurs to me that ultrasound should be able to tell us if the baby is a boy or a girl. I make a mental note to give Lin another exam once this test is done.

When the countdown on the screen reaches zero, I call Lin over.

"Buckle in," I tell her.

"Why?"

"Because I'm about to launch one of the transports, and there might be a jolt."

I have no idea if there will be a jolt or not, but I want her still and strapped in anyway. If there is a jolt, I don't want her abdomen banging against the wall of the control room. She sits and buckles up again, reaching over and placing her hand on my genitals.

"Lin," I say with a sigh, but I don't try to make her remove her hand. "Here goes nothing."

I click the launch button on the screen, but nothing happens. At least, it doesn't seem to until we see *Human Transport One* appear in the window, getting smaller as it approaches the planet. I pull up the transport ship's console on my screen and watch as the altitude ticks down. The destination coordinates are locked in, but the Artificial Intelligence is programmed to make any corrections just in case it looks like the ship might land hanging off a cliff or something.

The *Armstrong's* orbit causes the transport ship to disappear from view in the window, but I still have data coming in. The external hull temperature begins a rapid ascent as the ship enters the atmosphere. The speed relative to the planet's surface drops as rapidly as the altitude which reaches about 13,000 meters when the screen goes blank.

"What happened?" When I get no answer to that, I say, "Alexis, what happened?"

"*Human Transport One* is now out of range. The *Armstrong* will be able to reestablish contact on the next orbit in one hour and fourteen minutes."

I throw my hands up. "Great. How hard would it have been to equip the *Armstrong* with satellite relays that could be launched and stationed around the planet?"

"What?" Lin asks.

"Nothing," I say as I unbuckle my seat belt. "Come on, let's go home."

"I want to stay and float."

"I don't know if floating is good for the baby." To emphasize this, I caress her abdomen.

"Oh," she says and unbuckles her belt.

Hand in hand we float toward the airlock that leads back to the wheel section. Lin's hand has had an effect on me, but at least I can pretend that my erection is just my penis floating in zero gravity. Once through both airlock doors and back into what I think of as one of the spokes of the wheel, I manually disengage the airlock. I could do it remotely from the console, but if it didn't work, I'd have to come back here and do it manually anyway. We float back to the familiar control room of the wheel section, and I start the rotation to simulate gravity again. The sensation is a little like plunging down the first hill of a roller coaster, but that doesn't last long. Unlike the last time I reengaged gravity, I don't hear anything crashing to what is now the floor.

Once our orbit lines back up, I try connecting to the transport ship, hoping that it finished its landing. When the numbers appear on the screen, they all appear normal. The ship has landed, and the camera's have engaged. I pull up the feed from camera one and see the red and white chute flapping in the breeze.

"Thank God," I say, thinking that if this chute hadn't disintegrated, then the chutes in the other two transport ships hadn't either.

I switch to one of the other camera feeds and see a silver object above the high green grass undulating in the breeze.

"Lander 15," I say.

I zoom in and see that its solar panel has been broken off. That would explain why it hadn't sent anything up to the mother ship in several years. But it had been active for years before that. The question is, what had broken that solar panel?

25

I take Lin to the ultrasound after our next sleep cycle.

"We already did this," she says as she lies back on the table.

"I know. But it's good to keep checking to make sure the baby is growing OK."

I don't want to tell her my real reason for this check just in case I can't tell if the baby is a boy or a girl. After the training we had for this mission, I feel fairly confident I can read the ultrasound correctly, but that confidence diminishes when I see the snowy image on the screen. Still, I keep moving the wand around, making out the head and the arms.

"Turn around," I say.

Lin starts to sit up, and I put my other hand on her.

"Not you. Talking to the baby."

"The baby can hear you?"

"I doubt it," I say.

"Then why do you talk to him?"

"How do you know it's a "him"?

Right then, I see it, a perfect shot between the baby's legs. I move the wand around to make sure, but there it is, the penis and scrotum.

"I don't know," Lin says.

"You're right though. It is a boy."

"What?"

"Right there," I say, pointing to the genitalia on the screen.

"You sure?" Lin says.

"Pretty sure. If it were a girl, I wouldn't be so sure, but with a boy, everything is right out there."

I have frozen the screen so the image is still. Lin stares at it for a moment and then shrugs.

"I don't see it."

I point to the screen, showing her the shapes. Lin looks at it and looks down at me.

"Okay."

"You'll take my word for it," I finish for her.

"Yeah."

"All right."

I unfreeze the screen and finish a check. The baby is growing at the expected rate, and he looks as healthy as he can be.

The transport ships are each equipped with two drones, and I spend the next few weeks exploring what will probably be our future home. The three landing craft are designed to connect to each other and form a structure in which to live, but I can still change my mind if something about this site seems wrong. I only use one of the drones, saving the other as a backup, and fly it three miles in every direction from the transport ship. I keep Lin with me as much as I can, and she seems to pick up most of what I'm saying. I see no sign of that green cat creature that I saw in the old video taken by the landing probe, but I'm sure it and others are out there. To the east of the transport ship, the jungle is thick with thirty foot high trees and vegetation of a type I've never seen on earth. Most of the plants are bright green, as if they have all overdosed on chlorophyl.

It rains for an hour or two every other day, and the temperature range stays between 65 and 85 Fahrenheit, reminding me that it was the stats and video from this site that had prompted me to name the planet Eden all those weeks ago. Except for the camouflaged flying predators and the cat creatures, this really could be paradise.

We see no sign of any agriculture or of the humanoid creatures seen at the site of Lander 7. This site is on one of the other continents, so perhaps those humanoids really are limited to that part of the planet. If they live underground, it stands to reason that they may not be a seagoing civilization. There is a camera on the transport ship, and I point it up at the sky, watching it occasionally, trying to spot any sign of those blue pterodactyl-looking creatures. If they are present, their camouflage is so good that I can't spot them.

A river flows through the jungle area to the east, less than a mile from the transport ship, so we would have a water source if the rains stopped for whatever reason. There is a mountain range to the south, with the foothills just visible from the ground outside the transport ship. I can fly the drone high enough to see the snow covered peaks behind those foothills. The landing site is more than two hundred miles from the tidal flood plain and the ocean beyond, off to the west. We shouldn't have to worry about flooding from the tides, but on a planet with three moons, who can really tell for sure? The jungle is full of benign looking creatures, some of which look like a cross between mammals and small dinosaurs.

Once I've explored the site, I check out Lander 15. The shattered solar panel is on the ground next to it, broken off at the base near the probe itself. I have at least six years' worth of video from the probe, so this damage didn't happen during the landing. Perhaps some of the animals from the jungle did venture out and played on the solar panel, putting so much weight on it that it broke. But as the days and weeks of observing wear on, the more unlikely that becomes as I never see any of them more than a few feet outside of the jungle canopy.

After a month, I have a pretty good map of the entire area. I've even managed to get a sample of the water from the river. The lab in the transport ship has limited remote capabilities, but the river water tests with enough microorganisms that we would have to boil it before drinking. With the amount of rain the site is getting, we won't have to worry about going to the river for water very often if at all. There should be enough materials on board to create an adequate rain capture system to gather our drinking water.

During the fifth week after landing, a storm hits the

area. It lasts a full day, and at their worst, the wind speed measures at fifty-six miles an hour. The video feed shows a couple of lightning strikes in the jungle. A crash is heard after one of them, and I imagine a large portion of one of the giant trees crashing through the foliage to the ground. From orbit, the storm forms in a line of clouds that look like a front of some kind. I have seen cyclones, hurricane-like storms, over the oceans from orbit, but our site is far enough inland that I don't think we will have to worry about those.

"That's scary," Lin says when I zoom in on the loud lighting strike and play it again.

"It's just a thunderstorm. I grew up in Texas and then moved to South Dakota, so I'm used to them."

"Does that ever hit someone?"

"Lightning? Yeah, some people have been hit by lightning. Like on a golf course. But we won't be playing golf when we get to the planet."

"They die?" Lin asks, concern in her voice.

"Sometimes. But people have been known to survive. *The Guinness Book of World Records* listed one guy as having been struck by lightning seven times."

"He died?"

"Well, yeah, he's dead now. But the lightning strikes didn't kill him, no. He survived all seven of them."

"Wow."

She still looks worried, so I say, "We will stay indoors during storms. We'll be fine."

Lin gazes at the screen as footage of the storm continues to play on it. "Okay."

I pull her close and embrace her.

"We'll be fine. This is what we were sent out here for,

to go down there and make lots of babies and live our lives. It'll be an adventure. That's what life is, a big adventure."

I wish I feel as positive as I try to sound. We sit holding each other for a few minutes before Lin speaks again.

"I wish I could remember Earth like you do."

"I know."

"I watch the videos, and I see myself older and smarter and busy. The me from Earth did things. She knew things."

"Life is very different when you're part of a society of nine billion people. Out here, it's just us. We are supposed to start our own society. And maybe one day, this planet will get to nine billion people, all of them here because of us, because we did go down to the planet, because we kept living and exploring and didn't give up."

Lin is quiet for a few more minutes.

"I'm scared," she says.

"I know. I've been struggling with fear ever since I woke up here on the *Armstrong*. But we have to keep going. We can't stay up here. We were never meant to stay here. This ship zipped through space for over three billion years to find this planet right here for us to live on. That's the only reason we were—" I stop, not knowing what word to use. "Created," I finally come up with. "We were created to live down there, on that world."

"Get busy living, or get busy dying," Lin says, quoting a movie we had watched the other day.

"Exactly."

"Oh, hey!" Lin grabs my hand and puts it on her large abdomen.

"What?" I say, and then I feel it. The baby is kicking.

"See. He agrees. Get busy living." I leave the last part of the quote off.

26

Lin goes into labor in her 39th week. I am checking camera feeds from the other landers that still have working probes and cameras. I am committed to the site of *Human Transport One* as our settlement site, so I consider our last few weeks on the *Armstrong* as my last chance to explore the rest of the planet. Lin shuffles up to me at the console holding her belly.

"Are you all right?" I ask.

She shakes her head. "I had a pain."

"A pain?"

"Yeah."

"Does it still hurt?"

She pauses a few seconds before saying, "No."

We have been doing frequent examinations and checks

with the ultrasound since learning the sex of the baby, and everything has been normal so far. Lin has on more than one occasion treated the exam like foreplay which has been distracting as I'm always trying to at least pretend to be professional.

I stand up, take Lin by the hand, and lead her back to the ultrasound machine. Her walk is more like a waddle, but I have refrained from saying anything about it. She's only ever seen ducks on the video monitor, and I am reluctant to compare her to anything she has never actually seen.

"It could be contractions starting, but it could also be Braxton-Hicks," I say to her as we walk.

"What's that?"

"They're like contractions, but just of the uterus. Your cervix doesn't do anything."

"Is that bad?"

"No, it's normal. But if these are real labor contractions, we need to know it."

I help her up onto the table and do an exam. I'm not a doctor or even a medical professional by any measure, but it seems fairly obvious to me that her cervix is more open that it has been.

"OK, so maybe they weren't Braxton-Hicks."

"Is the baby coming?"

"It looks like it. It could be a long time yet though. We need to measure the time between contractions. Tell me the next time you have a pain, and I'll start a clock."

"Okay."

She lies back on the table looking at the rounded ceiling, and I see her bottom lip quiver.

"Hey, it'll be all right," I say, kissing her forehead and

stroking her cheek.

Lin takes my hand and kisses the back of it.

"Humans have been having babies for thousands of years," I tell her before realizing that this may be the first human birth in eons.

"What if the baby won't come out?" Lin asks.

"He'll come out. And if he doesn't, we have everything we need for a c-section." *Except for a doctor*, I think but don't say out loud.

We have, of course, seen videos of every kind of human childbirth, vaginal delivery, Cesarean section, breech birth, water delivery, premature birth, etc. More of our training for this mission was in childbirth than anything related to space flight. Propagation of the species was the sole reason we were out here.

I am probably more afraid of something going wrong than Lin is as I would have to perform whatever turns out to be necessary even with my limited training. Lilly Markum was supposed to have been the lead for all health and medical issues, but her clone had failed to grow just like the rest of the others.

"How do you feel right now?" I ask.

Lin shrugs. "Fine."

"All right, we go back to normal activity, but you let me know as soon as a pain hits."

I go back to the control room, but my heart isn't into planetary exploration anymore. I sit and stare at the frozen image on the screen. Lin goes back to the lounge, watching something with a laugh track on the video screen.

"Oh!" she yells a few minutes later.

"Contraction?"

"Yes."

I start a timer on the console screen and get up to see to Lin.

"Just stay there and keep breathing," I tell her.

An old sitcom plays on the screen, and I think that if one of the characters on that show were about to have a baby, the whole cast would comedically take the mom-to-be to the hospital. I am the hospital here on the *Armstrong*.

"Yuck," Lin says. "I think I peed."

I see the pool of liquid spread on the rubber floor between Lin's legs.

"That's not pee. Your water just broke."

"That bad?" Lin asks as she winces from the pain.

"No, it's normal. But it means things are about to get serious."

Lin lets out a deep exhale. "Okay, pain's over."

"Let's get you up and to the infirmary then."

The next twenty hours or so are spent monitoring Lin's and the baby's vital signs, timing her contractions, and checking to see how much Lin's cervix is dilated. I also play videos of Lilly Markum's childbirth training sessions on the screen. Lin always laughs whenever she sees Earth Kevin or Earth Linda on the screen whether she's in the middle of a contraction or not.

Lin is able to sleep for a while between contractions, but I can't look away. Luckily, one of the plants that survived three billion years on ice is coffee bean, so I am wired on caffeine. Once she's dilated to about nine centimeters, I run the ultrasound paddle over her. The baby is head down, and umbilical cord appears to be far away from his neck.

"I'm tired," Lin says with a whine.

"We're almost there. Just a few more contractions should do it."

She sighs just before tensing with another long contraction. I hold her hand through it and check her again.

"We're close enough," I tell her.

I look around and make sure I have everything I might need within reach. Lin's face is covered in sweat, and her hair sticks to both cheeks. Her eyes are closed like she's giving up and going to sleep.

"Lin, it's time to push now."

"Push now," she mumbles.

"Yes, you have to push like you are trying to poop and pee at the same time and everything is stuck. Can you do that?"

She doesn't open her eyes, but she does lean forward with what appears to be a half-hearted attempt at a push.

"OK, that was the first one. You have to do better with the next one."

"I'll make a mess."

"That's all right. I'll clean it up later. It'll have to be me because you'll be busy with the baby." I take both her hands in mine. "You hear me. The baby is ready to come out now. Are you ready for that?"

Lin opens her eyes and nods. I pull her upper body forward while urging her to push. She does with a yell, and I talk her down after about a half a minute. We do this several times before I can see the head.

"Almost there," I say. "Only one or two more."

I don't take her hands this time, anticipating having to catch my son. Once his head gets clear, the rest of him almost falls out into my arms. His skin is gray, and he is quiet. I put him in the fold of my left arm and use the bulb syringe to clear his mouth and nostrils. His hands flail, trying to defend himself, and he finally inhales and then lets out a strong throaty cry. Lin is suddenly awake, her eyes wide as she stares at the baby.

"Here he is," I say, lying him on her chest.

He immediately opens his mouth as if looking for a nipple. I help Lin move him over so he can latch on. I watch my new son with his mother, thinking that this is why I am here in this universe. My vision blurs before I feel the tears falling down my cheeks. I shake my head, knowing that there are still things to do. I cut and clamp the umbilical cord and then tell Lin that she has to push the placenta out. She looks at me like I have three heads.

"Come on, baby," I say, positioning a tray beneath her to catch everything.

She manages to push it out. It looks like a special effects thing from a horror movie. I set it aside and kiss Lin's forehead.

"You did great," I say.

"I'm tired."

"I know. Do you want me to take the baby?"

She looks down at him, suckling at her breast, and shakes her head.

"What's his name?" Lin asks.

"We need to decide that?"

"We give him a name?"

"That's the way it usually works."

Lin looks down at him. "I don't know any names. What would be a good name for him?"

My first thought was Adam since he was the first baby born in this system. But I decide against it. If we are going to start this new civilization, we don't need to stick with the old world. And I don't want to name him after any of Earth Kevin's kids. Let their memories live inside me without conflicts with this new world.

"How about Hal?" I say without any consideration for where I pull that name from. I had been thinking that we were in a spaceship, and I spoke as soon as the thought of the Hal computer from the movie *2001: A Space Odyssey* entered my head. "Never mind," I say before Lin can open her mouth.

"Hal," she says to the baby, and I realize it's too late to take it back.

"You sure?"

"Yes. Hal. Hi Hal. I'm Lin."

Well, why not? Hal has three letters just like Kev and Lin. Maybe that can be a tradition in our family.

"You should have him call you Mommy."

She looks at me, her face seeming to glow with radiance. "Mommy," she repeats.

When I finally get Hal away from Lin to examine him, he weighs six pounds, two ounces. He seems perfectly healthy, with ten fingers, ten toes, a bit of dark hair on his head, and two bright blue eyes. Lin drops to sleep almost immediately. I find one of the bassinets that were included in our supplies, and I tear open another of the vacuum packed bags of blankets. Once I get Hal settled, I carry Lin to her own bed and then move the bassinet so that it sits next to her. Once I've done everything I needed to do, exhaustion hits me like a lead weight. I crawl into the bed next to Lin and go to sleep myself.

27

Hal loses almost half a pound over the next few days as Lin has trouble getting her milk to produce. We have a bunch of baby formula, but I don't know how nourishing it would be after all the time in space. We watch all of the videos on breast feeding in the ship's library, implement some of the techniques, and things start to open up. Hal gains back the weight he lost and adds to it. His face fills out, and his eyes turn from blue to dark brown. He sleeps a lot in short stints, and wakes up every two hours or so to eat. Lin, who had been used to sleeping in long stretches, seems to be tired and sleepy all the time. We are like a typical couple with a newborn, and I sometimes almost forget that we are practically the only human beings in the universe. Even if there are others out there in the vast expanse, we couldn't possibly live long enough for the trip to meet up with them. The only other humans Lin and I will ever see in our lives are the ones we conceive and raise. I don't know if that thought is frightening or comforting, but it is undeniably true.

It had occurred to me before, but it really hits me now, looking at Hal in the flesh, that for the human species to survive on this planet, our children will have to intermarry, to have sex with each other. I tell myself to throw out my moral objections to it, that in the Bible, Adam and Eve's children would have had to do the same thing. Come to think of it, the Bible only ever mentions three sons of Adam and Eve: Cain, Abel, and Seth, and zero daughters, almost as if they didn't count. Cain, of course, killed Abel and was cast out. After that, he just magically had a wife who bore him sons. Where did his wife come from if Adam and Eve were the first man and woman? Did he take one of his sisters when he was banished? Or were there people on the planet other than Adam and Eve? If it were a novel or a movie, it would be a huge plot hole, if the Bible can be said to have had a plot.

At the time the book of Genesis was written, women were treated as commodities, necessary for the bearing of sons. Did that mean the writers didn't feel that mentioning them in the genealogies was worth the effort?

I figure that the odds of a human civilization surviving for any significant length of time on the planet below are miniscule. We will be in danger of extinction for generations, hundreds of years. We have to be fruitful and multiply as God told Adam and Eve in Genesis. Yes, each female will have to bear as many children as possible, but that doesn't mean that females have to be treated as commodities. Perhaps we should set up a matriarchal system, basing our names and genealogies on mothers instead of fathers.

Lin is sleeping now as I walk around the wheel section with the baby. Hal is sleeping too, but I don't want to put him down just yet. When I pass Lin's bed, I stop and look at her, gently bouncing Hal so that he still has the feeling of movement. Lin lies on her side, her face toward me. Her belly has been shrinking, but it's still not back to its pre-pregnancy shape. I can see stretch marks on her hips, and I think about what a miracle she and Hal are. Since Lin's memory download didn't work, she has had to learn everything at lightning speed. Somehow, she did that. She speaks like an adult now; she can do most chores; and she can run most of the ship's processes. If something happened to me, she could even follow the procedures for getting in the transport ship and going down to the planet, even though she says that she'd still rather stay on the ship and float in zero gravity on occasion.

She can only read on a second grade level, but with the voice commands, reading hasn't been a priority. Reading will probably never be a priority for her. Once we move to the planet, the priorities will be surviving and raising a family, preferably a large one. If, by some miracle, the human race survives the first few hundred years on this planet, Lin is a name that should be revered. She would literally be the mother of all mankind.

Hal's stirs in my arms, and his face scrunches up.

"Shhh," I say, increasing the bouncing, but it's a lost cause.

He wakes up and lets out an angry, hungry cry. Lin's

eyes spring open, and she reaches for him. I hand him to her, and he frantically digs his face into her breast until he finds what he's looking for.

"I pulled one of the breast pumps out of storage," I say.

"Why?" Lin asks.

"Because I'd like to feed Hal too. It's good that you have bonded so well with him, but I'd like to experience a bit of that."

We already have a good supply of bottles and rubber nipples that had been stored with more of the day to day items.

"Plus, it would take some of the pressure off you," I add. "We pump your breasts, store the milk, and then I could feed him. Let you sleep more than two hours at a time."

Lin looks off into the space behind me as if thinking about how nice it would be to sleep eight hours in a row again.

"Okay," she says.

"Of course, Hal will have to stop eating long enough to let you pump."

"He eats a lot?"

I nod. "He seems to. My other kids were the same way though."

Lin frowns and looks at me.

"Well, they're not *my* other kids. Earth Kevin's."

Lin remains quiet and nods. While she seems mollified, I can't help but feel like I'm betraying Thomas, Kaitlyn, and Bobby by not claiming them as my own. My brain tells me they've been gone for billions of years, but the memories of them are so clear and fresh. Will I ever get to a point where my real memories become distinct from the ones that were artificially implanted into my head?

"I'm going back to work," I tell Lin. Maybe resuming my planetary exploration will clear my mind. "Holler if you need anything."

She nods and looks back down at Hal who seems to have drifted back into sleep even as he continues feeding.

28

I keep exploring the site of our future home with the drones on the transport ship, and it continues to look idyllic. There is a storm that blows through when Hal is nine weeks old. Temperatures get down to sixty-seven degrees Fahrenheit, with three and one quarter inches of rain and a top wind gust of forty-six miles an hour. Other than that, the sun keeps shining, and the afternoon showers keep coming every other day or so. Thanks to the night vision camera on one of the drones, I see a lot of nocturnal activity around the landing site. Several of the cat-like creatures sniff around the edge of the transport's landing pads. One of them bolts after a smaller creature that looks like a cross between a squirrel and a kangaroo. I can't get a good look at it because it moves too fast. My video captures of it just reveal a brown blur.

Once on the planet, we will be living inside the transport ships. They are designed to be bound together and form a much larger structure. We can deploy wheels to move them next to each other to complete this set up. I'm debating whether to go down with the second transport or send it down unmanned and take the third one. I don't deliberate on it for long. It would be tragic to send the second ship down and then have something prevent the third transport ship from launching out of the *Armstrong*. No, we will take the second ship, sooner rather than later. I long to see a sky and open spaces.

The original mission plan had been for us to live in orbit for at least a year, and we have done that. Each transport is equipped with six adult seats and four child seats. The six adults were supposed to go down to the planet two at a time, but Jordan built in extra seats in case something went wrong with one or more transports. Since it's just Lin and me, along with Hal, we should have plenty of room for our trip down. The seatbelts are encased in plastic like the ones at the console, so they stayed intact during the long trip.

I check the hard drive storage space on Transport Two and see that everything is intact. The drives on the transports serve as backups for the main drives on the *Armstrong*, so all the shows and videos we have on board will be accessible on the planet for as long as our view screens remain operational. There is a library of wilderness survival videos that we haven't accessed yet since there has been no need while we are still in orbit. Of course, those survival videos were all shot on Earth, and conditions will be different on Eden.

I walk through our garden checking all the fruits and vegetables. In another week, we will be at a point where a harvest will bring the most reward. Most of the crops would then have to either be replanted or recycled. It would be the best time over the next three months to leave for the surface. Just seven more days.

I find Lin on the floor of the lounge breastfeeding Hal and watching one of Earth Linda's personal videos, taken when she was in her late thirties.

"Why do you keep watching those?" I ask, sitting down beside her.

Lin shrugs. "I just like watching this other me sometimes."

I put my hand on her thigh. She looks at me, smiles, and lays her head on my shoulder. We had resumed our sexual activities about five weeks after Hal was born.

"I think it's time to go," I say.

"Now?" Lin looks alarmed.

"No. One more week. Seven days. We'll pick the crops that are ready, load up the rest of the supplies, and go down to the planet."

Lin sighs and sits back up. She pulls Hal from her breast. Hal cries at this until Lin gets him turned around and on her other breast.

"You said when we leave, we can never come back here?"

"Yes, that's right."

She looks up and around, the curved ceiling, the walls just a few yards from each other. Except for the excursion to the cylinder section, we have been in this circular tube for over a year. It's all that Lin remembers.

"We get to float for a while before we go?"

I laugh. "Yes, we'll get to float over to the cylinder section like we did last time. I'll be going back and forth, loading supplies before we leave."

"Hal will like it."

"Yeah. Too bad he won't remember it when he's older."

"He won't?"

"No, he's a baby. Do you remember when you woke up here the first time, and I found you on the floor?"

Lin takes a moment to think. "No. Why don't I remember?"

"You didn't know how to talk. You didn't have a sense of self. Just like Hal. But your brain was already developed, so you learned fast."

Lin nods and gazes down at Hal. On the screen, thirty-something year old Earth Linda stands in front of the United States Capitol in Washington D.C., talking about a lecture she was scheduled to give at Georgetown University later that day.

"I feel like I will miss this place," she says. "But I'm ready to see something else. Like what I see in the videos."

I look at the Capitol, at the people walking by behind Earth Linda.

"It won't be like that. That world is long gone. But it is now up to us to start a new one."

I have concerns about exposing Hal to zero gravity so young. His skull on the top of his head is still developing. As of the time the six *Armstrongs* left Earth, no study of the effects of zero gravity on the development of young children had ever been done. So my fears might be unfounded, but I decide to limit his exposure to it. The day before our departure is spent in furious activity. I move all of the vacuum wrapped supplies, toilet paper, diapers, formula, etc., from the storage area to just outside the door to the spoke that we will use to get to the cylinder section. Most of these supplies will be put in the third transport ship which I will launch toward the planet surface remotely once we are there, but some of it will go in the ship with us. Lin and I reap the harvest of our little garden, packing up all the fruit and vegetables and other food to go with us to the surface. I had spent the previous five days manufacturing as many steaks as the 3-D printer could produce.

Once everything is staged, Lin and I eat a big dinner and then try to relax in the lounge. It feels like a calm before the storm. Hal is awake and lying on his belly on the floor between us. We watch him stretch for the rubber pretzel that he likes to play with. When he gets it, he rolls over onto his back as he puts it in his mouth and starts gnawing on it.

"He'll be getting teeth soon," I say.

"Oh," Lin says and touches her two nipples with the palms of her hands.

"Sorry," I say.

"It'll be OK. I love him."

We look at each other and smile. I look away and all around us.

"Last night on this ship," I say.

Lin nods, and a tear falls down her cheek.

"Don't cry," I say.

She shakes her head and wipes it away. "I'm excited,

but I'm also sad that we can never come back here. I've never been anywhere else."

"I know."

Hal takes the pretzel out of his mouth, looks at it, and puts it back in.

"I need to sleep tonight," I say. "Tomorrow's a big day."

"I will make sure his belly is full so he will sleep longer."

She gets to her feet then bends down and picks Hal up, putting him to her breast. I stand up and head toward the bed.

29

I wake up even before the *Armstrong's* lights automatically power on. Hal is not in his bassinet next to the bed, and Lin is nowhere to be found. I walk through the wheel section to her old room, where I first found her on the floor. She is sleeping in the pod where her body was conceived and grown to adulthood. Her last night was spent here where she started it. Hal is sleeping against her, one nipple near his mouth, but he seems to have lost the connection in his sleep.

I hate to wake them up, but I've done everything that can be done with the wheel section turning. The next thing I need to do is turn off the gravity, and Lin needs to be awake when that happens. I'm about to shake her shoulder when the lights click on. They are dim at first as they are programmed to power up gradually, simulating a sunrise.

"Lin, it's time," I say, shaking her shoulder.

She stirs, looks at me with sleepy, unfocused eyes. When she sees me, she bolts upright, suddenly awake. Hal, still asleep, rolls toward the spot where she had lain, and she jumps up off the bed and gently scoops him up. We walk over to the control room. I think to myself that the next time we walk, it will be on the planet surface.

"I'll move most of the stuff," I tell Lin. "You just watch Hal. And if he appears to be having any trouble, tell me right away."

"What, trouble?"

"Just anything. Zero gravity might affect him somehow."

"Okay."

I take a deep breath and say, "Alexis, stop the gravity spin."

"Stopping gravity spin."

I turn and hurry over to the spoke we are going to use and all the stuff I placed at the entrance. Some of it is velcro'ed to the wall, but some of it will start floating as soon as the wheel rotation stops. Once I get there, I have to wait a few more minutes for the gravity to be completely gone. I don't want to have to push any of these big boxes up a ladder, so I wait until there is no up or down. I take the floating boxes first, pushing four of them into the tube and float in after them, pushing them all the way into the cylinder section.

It takes me over four hours to get everything moved and stored on the two transport ships. I enter the cockpit of Transport Two to start running its diagnostics. Once they are started, I check the console storage and find a Bible. I pick it up and thumb through it. Amazingly, all the pages are intact. The thin, almost tissue-like paper of its pages somehow evaded the disintegration of most of our other paper products. The name on the inscription page just behind the front cover says *Kacey Thomas*, Presented by *Your Father with Love*, and Date *May 28, 2029*. It is a thick ESV Study Bible, although there aren't any notes or marks that I can see upon first glance. There are supposed to be six iterations of the *Armstrong*, each with three transport ships. Out of 18 transport ships, I happen to choose the one that contains Kacey's Bible.

"Is this another sign God?" I ask aloud, but I am met with silence.

I wish I could see outside, just to make sure there isn't a silver triangle zipping around in orbit over the planet. I place the Bible back in its place and continue checking the diagnostics, which takes another hour. All systems are go.

"Well, okay," I say to nobody.

There is nothing left to do except launch the transport. I check our position in orbit against our landing site and see I only have forty-five minutes left until a launch window. It's time to get Lin and Hal.

I float back to the wheel section and find them in the lounge, floating in front of the screen, which is playing an old Pixar movie. I stop and watch for a couple of minutes. Lin lets go of Hal and watches him kick in the air, the movie on the screen mostly ignored. When Hal gets frustrated because he can't go where he wants, he starts to fuss, and Lin grabs him and talks to him in a soothing voice. When he's calm, she lets go of him again and the scene replays itself. Lin spots me when she goes to grab him this time.

"It's time," I say.

She nods. I reach over and pull her close to the wall so that she can grab the rail and move herself along the circle section. We pull ourselves through a complete lap around without saying anything, our way of saying goodbye to our home. Lin has tears floating in front of her face when we stop at the hatch to the spoke that we will use to move to the cylinder section.

"One chapter ends, and another begins," I say.

"I know."

We take one last look at the curving ceiling and floor where we have spent the last year and a half and head up the spoke to the cylinder section. We float into the control room, huge compared to anything in the wheel section, and look out the window at the blue, white, and green planet below.

"It's beautiful," Lin says.

"Yes, it is. It's home now. For better or worse."

The countdown on the console screen has dropped below five minutes. Once that countdown ends, we will have a window of about ten minutes to launch out of the *Armstrong*. I take Lin by the hand and pull her with me toward Transport Two. She has decided to hold Hal during the descent rather than strap him into one of the child seats.

"He will be scared and scream the whole way," she had said to me when we had talked about it the day before.

If Lin was going to refuse the child seat for him, part of me wants to be the one holding him. I have memories of Earth re-entry, so I know the kind of g-forces that we will be feeling. But I gave in when I saw the way she had held onto him when we talked about it. After we push and pull ourselves into the transport, I close and lock the hatch and get Lin and Hal strapped in, making sure that the belt goes over Hal's back, holding him in place on Lin's chest. I take the seat next to them and strap myself in just as the countdown goes to zero. It is replaced by another one which starts at 9:53 and continues down.

In every launch I have ever witnessed or been a part of, there was always a Mission Control coordinating every aspect of the mission. It seems strange that I am not calling CAPCOM somewhere and asking for a go/no go order. But Mission Control no longer exists. It is just Lin and me and our baby, alone in the vast universe. I flip a couple of switches on the console, and the big red button in front of me turns green. I press it, and we hear a sucking sound as the bay doors open and the bay quickly depressurizes. Once the door is fully open, the transport ship jerks forward and shoots out of the *Armstrong*. Lin and I look out the window above us. Once we get a bit further away, we can see the entire ship, the large cylinder section in the middle with three bell shaped engines on one end and long solar panels at the other end, perpendicular to the cylinder section. The wheel section is around the cylinder section, a little closer to the solar panels than to the engines. It is still now, but we can still see light in the small windows.

The artificial intelligence has plotted a course and has full control of the transport ship, although we are not so much flying as falling. I can just see a small sliver of the planet out the front window. Thrusters fire occasionally, pointing the heat shield toward the oncoming atmosphere of the planet. I glance over to Lin. I want to take her hand, but she has both arms wrapped around Hal.

"I love you Lin," I say.

She looks at me and forces a smile. "Love you too."

I give a silent prayer to a God that I once thought probably never ventured this far away from Earth. I've since reconsidered after finding Kacey's Bible intact on, of all Transport ships, this one, the one we are taking down to the planet. My hands grip the arm rests of my seat. The figures on the console tell me that we are falling at over 24,000 miles per hour. In space though, all "speed" is relational. That 24,000 miles per hour is just in relation to the planet below us. That number starts decreasing before I feel any resistance. Heat shield temperature appears on another screen, and that number starts rising as soon as it appears. It feels as though my body is being pulled to the ceiling as it strains against the straps across my chest. I look over to make sure Hal is all right, that he isn't being crushed between the seat belt and his mother. He is awake and crying, but I can barely hear him over the roar of the atmospheric friction against the transport ship. The floor seems to vibrate, and I can only imagine the heat shield splitting in two, the fires shooting through the ship and engulfing us all. I close my eyes, not wanting to see death take us. The vibration strengthens, and the roar keeps getting louder and louder.

This is taking too long. How are we not dead? But when the roar begins to lessen, I open my eyes and look at the console. The heat shield temperature is decreasing. Our speed is now below one thousand miles per hour and still dropping. I can hear Hal crying. Lin is patting his back now that the G-forces aren't trying to pull us out of our chairs. Just when I'm feeling good about our situation, we hear something like a shotgun blast, and the entire ship jerks. I look out the upper window and see the parachute has opened. By the time I look back at the screen, our speed is under one hundred miles per hour and still dropping. Because of the angle of the ship and our windows, we can't see down. Our altitude shows us at just over two thousand feet and falling slowly now.

"I think the worst is over," I tell Lin.

She looks at me, eyes red. She has been crying, probably thinking, like me, that we were going to die. Hal has stopped crying, but he looks at me like I am a crazy man.

"Aw, Hal, I'm sorry," I say, reaching over and caressing his cheek.

"I want to go home," Lin says.

"I know. We're almost there. To our new home, that is."

Lin looks up at the window, at the billowing parachute above us. I feel the thrusters firing on one side of the ship, moving us in a certain direction. The artificial intelligence has control of the ship and is taking us in for a landing, hopefully next to that first transport ship.

"Can I take this off now?" Lin asks, her hand on the release for her seat belt.

"I think so."

She unbuckles it and moves Hal to her left breast. He frantically connects and begins eating like he had been starved. I unbuckle my own seat belt, stand up, and lean forward to look out the lower window. I can see the tops of trees in the distance, but I can't see our landing site. Sitting back down, I see that our altitude is three hundred feet. Thrusters fire again, altering our descent. We barely feel the impact of our landing, and I'm not even sure we have landed until the parachute collapses above our upper window. I hear the vents open, depressurizing the cabin and letting in air from the outside.

Are we the first human beings to ever breathe natural air on a planet or celestial body other than Earth? "I wonder…"

"What?" Lin asks.

I tell her what I was thinking. She shrugs. "Who knows?"

"Nobody. And that's the thing. We will never know what happened to the rest of the human race."

I stand on wobbly legs, and open the hatch on the port side as it is the one displaying a green light. Bright sunlight floods inside, and we squint until our eyes adjust as the stairs automatically deploy from the bottom of the hatch to the ground about ten feet below us. I hear Lin take a deep breath behind me.

"Welcome to Wonderland," I say to her.

30

I step carefully out of the transport ship and onto the top stair. There are no handrails, so I go down a few more steps and turn to make sure Lin, carrying Hal, is able to make it safely down. When we get to the bottom two steps, I think about saying something profound like what Neil Armstrong had intended to say, "That's a small step for a man but a giant leap for Mankind." Of course, he didn't get the line exactly the way he wanted it, leaving out the "a" in front of man, but he also knew there were billions of people watching and listening to him. There is no such scrutiny here, but something comes to my mind anyway, a charge given by God to Adam and Eve in the Bible that seems to sum up our entire mission here.

"May we be fruitful and multiply," I say as my foot hits

the ground.

I turn and help Lin down.

"It's so green," she says, looking around.

The warm breeze caresses our bodies, reminding us that, like Adam and Eve, we are naked. The grass we are standing in is almost knee high, the soil soft underneath our feet. Lin looks up, face to the blue sky. A few wispy white clouds float by high above us. To our right, off in the distance, is the jungle canopy with its strange noises. To our left is what appears to be an endless expanse of the gently rolling grass with various small trees scattered in the distance. Just ahead of us, about two hundred yards away, is the remains of probe lander 15 with its broken solar panel. We will have to take a look at that, but that can wait. It has been there for almost twenty years, after all, and it's not going anywhere. I take a deep breath of alien air, thinking that if all our instruments are wrong and the air is toxic, better to get everything over with now. Nothing happens as I exhale just as deeply.

Tears are streaming down Lin's face again, and I reach up to my own face and find tears of my own.

"Feels like we've been released from prison," I say.

"It's so big. So beautiful," Lin says.

Hal is oblivious, still nursing at his mother's breast. I reach over and caress his head. He pauses his suckling to look at me, almost in irritation at interrupting his meal. I can't help but laugh through my tears.

"Come on," I say to Lin. "Let's check out our transport ship."

I lead the way around the perimeter of our landing site. The parachute has fallen over the other side of the ship, partially covering Transport One next to us. It appears that the AI landed our Transport Two right next to the first one, exactly as designed. All we will have to do is remove the starboard wall from Transport Two and the port wall from Transport One to have an expanded living space.

We both high step through the grass as it tickles our legs. I hope there are no allergens in them. It would be our luck to land in the middle of grass that acts like poison ivy. We ought to be more careful, I think, but then I ask myself why. We are here on this planet forever, for better or worse. I think of the *Apollo 11* astronauts in quarantine after returning from the moon in a documentary I saw a long time ago, and it hits me again that Earth is gone. I am never going home. This is home now. I stop and go down on one knee.

"Are you all right?" Lin asks.

"Yeah," I say. "The weight of everything hits me every once in a while."

She puts her hand on my head, runs her fingers through my hair. I take a few more deep breaths and rise to my feet. We walk all the way around the two transport ships. I'll have to climb up and remove the two parachutes before I can deploy the solar panels and get power to our new home. We can cut up the chute and make seat covers, sheets, towels, or even clothes, but it's so warm here, and we've been naked for so long that I don't see the point in making anything wearable.

A mountain range is visible from the other side of Transport One. When I launch Transport Three, it should land here on the other side of the first transport, giving us a lot of interior space, along with all the supplies I packed in that ship.

Lin and I are covered in sweat by the time we get all

the way around the two ships.

"I have a lot of work to do," I say.

"I can help."

"I know. But you have to take care of Hal too."

We sit on the steps, neither of us wanting to go back inside. We've been inside for years, and this open sky is so majestic. The textured step soon becomes uncomfortable on our backsides, and we stand back up. There's so much to do, but I'm so tired. I don't even know what time of day it is. The sun is directly above us, so I have to guess that it's close to noon. Transport Two will run its air conditioner on battery power for several more hours.

"I need a nap," I say to Lin.

She smiles and nods, so we head back inside. A large bed has been built into the back wall of the cargo area. I have to move the supplies into the cockpit to be able to get the bed deployed, so I am even more exhausted by the time I am able to lie down. Lin and Hal, who is already sleeping, lie down next to me.

"Alexis," I say and wait for the ding. "Start keeping track of each day, with today as day one. I'll figure out an actual calendar later."

"Yes, Kev. Today is day one. Yesterday, your last day on the *Armstrong* is now day negative one. Is that how you want to count them?"

"Yes. Thank you."

I kiss Lin and try to go to sleep, but it takes a while.

It's dark when I wake up. Lin and Hal are not lying next

to me. I struggle to my feet, feeling a pressure in my head. I walk to the front, what used to be the cockpit. The supplies are stacked up on the chairs and console. Lin sits at the edge of the open hatch, her feet on the top steps.

"Hey there," I say.

"Hi. Did you sleep good?"

"I think so. I don't know. I feel strange."

"Yeah. Me too."

I sit next to her and see Hal sleeping in her arms. I look out into the darkness, which is not so dark. I see two moons in the sky, one full and one at the half stage. The full moon is the smaller one. Or maybe it's not. The one with the furthest orbit is actually the larger moon. It would just look smaller from the planet.

"That must be it," I say.

"What?"

"The *Armstrong* simulated only the gravitational pull of the planet. It didn't take into account the effect the three moons would have on it. That must be why we feel weird."

I pause, looking out at the shadows in the dark.

"Or, maybe it's just because we're no longer inside a spinning wheel," I add.

"Everything is different," Lin says.

"Yeah."

We sit in silence, listening to the sounds of the night. I hear a shrill shriek from somewhere deep in the jungle.

"What was that?" Lin asks, and Hal stirs in her arms.

"I don't know. Maybe one of those green cat things." I reach out and take Hal from her, putting his head on my shoulder and patting his back with what I hope is a heartbeat rhythm. He settles back down into sleep.

"I'm scared," Lin says.

"Yeah. I am too."

"Can we close this door?"

I gaze out into the semi darkness. The grass undulates in the wind. We hear another shriek from the jungle.

"Sure."

Lin gets to her feet and helps me up. It's more difficult for me since I have Hal, but I manage.

"Alexis," I say, "Close the hatch."

Below us, the stairs retract. Once they are in, the door slides shut. I lay Hal in the bassinet and go back to bed. Lin lies down beside me, and I hold her for a few minutes which soon turns into more vigorous activity.

31

Bright sunlight streams in when I awaken. Lin is next to me, and Hal is crying. It sounds more urgent than his normal hungry cry. I roll over Lin before she can get up and stagger over to get him. He clutches at me, pinching the skin on my shoulder. The strange feeling I had last night is still here.

"You're okay," I whisper to him, bouncing and patting him. "Did you have a bad dream?"

Lin stands beside me now, looking at Hal's face. His wails have turned to soft sobs. Lin holds her hands out, and I hand him over. She puts him to her breast, and that quiets him. She gives me a look of desperation.

"It'll be all right," I tell her. "We just have to adjust to life here."

Lin turns away from me and lies back down. I go to the console and see that our battery power is under 50%. We need to get the third transport here so that I can deploy the large solar panels that should power our "house" for years to come. The next launch window is a little over an hour from now. That doesn't give me enough time to clear the parachutes out of the way and arrange our supplies outside the two ships that are already here, just in case of a disaster with the landing of that third one. The next window is just after nightfall tonight, so that's the one I will shoot for.

I head back to our new bedroom, nodding to Lin as she continues nursing Hal. On the back wall is a closet with weapons. I open it and find three rifles and two handguns fastened to the wall. I take one of the handguns, a Glock 26, because I have memories of owning one just like it in South Dakota. It shoots 9 millimeter cartridges. The magazine in the gun is empty, so I grab a box of ammunition from the drawer below where the guns are stored, sit down at the edge of the bed, and start pushing cartridges into it.

"What's that?" Lin asks.

"It's a gun," I say. "In case anything attacks while I'm outside."

"Why are you going outside?"

"I've got to clear the parachutes and move some of our supplies out of here, just in case."

"Just in case what?"

"In case the third ship doesn't land right and crashes into these two. We don't want to lose everything we have. Although most of it is on that third ship."

I squeeze the last cartridge into the magazine and look

up at her. She has a look of utter fear on her face.

"It'll be all right," I say. "These two ships landed just fine."

"I want to go back," Lin says.

I shake my head. "We can't. I told you this was a one way trip."

"This place is scary. All those sounds."

I slam the magazine into the Glock and pull the slide back, chambering a round. Holding the gun up, I say, "We are scarier than anything out there. Believe me."

I pat her thigh and stand up. Lin watches silently as I head out, pausing to wait for the door to slide open and the stairs to extend down to the ground. Once I get outside, it occurs to me that the gun may not fire. It has spent three billion years in a zero gravity vacuum. There was nothing that could affect the gunpowder in the rounds, but three billion years is three billion years. I point the gun toward the grassy plain, pointed slightly down, and squeeze the trigger. The pop is loud but not deafening, and I see a bit of grass and dirt fly up where the bullet hits. I walk over to where it hit and nudge the broken soil with my toe.

"What was that?" Lin calls from the open hatch of the ship.

"I was testing the gun. It works." *Thank God.*

Lin, still holding Hal, looks around at the morning, sighs, and turns back inside. I walk back to the ships and around to the back where the chute sits over the top of Transport One, flapping in the breeze. I don't have a holster for the gun as I'm not wearing anything, so I have to climb up one handed. The ladder rungs on the side of the ship make this much easier than it otherwise would have been.

When I get up top, I find the chute's suspension lines in a tangled mess. I leave the gun up top, climb down, go back into the ship to get a knife, and climb back up to the roof. I cut the suspension lines and watch the chute blow away. It catches on one of the small trees in the distance. I leave it as I turn my attention to the chute from Transport One. Our second ship landed on top of part of it, so I am only going to be able to get part of the material. As I am about to go to work cutting the suspension lines connecting the chute to the first ship, the sound of the wind changes. I look up, and movement in the sky above me catches my eye. I see it, one of the blue dragon shaped things swooping down toward me. Its body is the same color as the sky, but the claws on its talons are black and sharp and coming right toward me. I drop down, rolling on the roof of the ship grabbing the Glock just as soon as I can reach it. I roll over one more time so that I'm on my back, raise the Glock, and fire all around those black claws. Chunks of the creature, red and pulpy, fly away with each bullet hit, and it flies past me, smacking the edge of the roof I'm on and crashing to the ground.

The thing's blue body is now very visible against the green grass, and I fire four more rounds into it as it tries to rise. The shots knock it back down, and it ceases all movement. I turn the gun skyward again, looking for any more movement. If Lin can't hear my rolling around on the roof, she could certainly hear the shots fired.

"Close the door!" I yell, hoping she can hear my voice. And then I wonder if the AI can hear it. "Alexis, close the door!"

I hear the stairs retract as I keep scanning the sky. How

many shots did I fire, and how many rounds do I still have left? I put seventeen in, one test shot, and at least nine shots at the thing. Maybe seven left. Maybe fewer than that. I might have fired ten or twelve at the thing. I had been in a panic, squeezing the trigger over and over. Hell, I'm still in a panic, looking for anything moving in the sky. The metal roof is hot from sitting under the sun all morning, burning the skin on my back and buttocks, but I'm afraid to move.

There's no movement above. Either this thing was alone, or any companions it had have left the scene. I jump up, hoping my skin hasn't fused to the roof. The blue creature hasn't moved. My skin is sore, but it's still on my body and not attached to the metal surface. I stumble over to the side and climb down, missing one of the bottom rungs of the ladder and falling onto my ass. Immediately, I roll, pointing the gun at the thing. I can't see much of it through the knee high grass, but what little I can see remains still. I stand on shaky legs, looking above me but keeping the gun pointed toward the thing on the ground and creep over to it. It appears to be on its back, eyes and mouth open. The eyes are black, the mouth lined with multiple rows of sharp teeth. I shoot it again, right between those two eyes just to make sure it's dead. Its body is about four feet long, but the wingspan is closer to twelve. The wings are just thin membranes with thick skeletal-looking lines running across it every three feet or so, kind of like a giant bat's wings. There are two limbs sticking up from its belly, each with three finger things tipped with those black claws. The skin and membranes are the same shade of blue as the sky, and I wonder if that's the only color this thing can be or if it would change to green when it's in the grass like this. It's dead now, so I'm pretty sure it couldn't change now, even if it ever could.

I want to cut this thing up, see if the meat is edible, but I left my knife on the roof. I climb back up and get it, keeping the Glock in one hand and my head on a swivel searching for any movement in the blue sky. The clouds are starting to arrive, so if these things are blue all the time, they should be easier to spot. I climb down a second time, this time without falling, which is a good thing since I have to carry the knife between my teeth. I need to make some kind of belt so I can wear the gun in a holster on my hip, although I will probably look ridiculous as a barefoot and hatless naked cowboy. Of course, there's no one here other than myself to think I look ridiculous. Lin and Hal won't care.

32

The meat of the blue bat thing is difficult to cut and, after cooking, even more difficult to chew. After months of simulated meat printed out of protein filaments, it tastes delicious though. I grill the meat in our kitchen, part of Transport Two. I had cut the wing membranes up and stretched them out to dry in the sun, which is now setting. I am trying to tan the rest of the skin, spread out and stretched in the sun next to the wing membranes, by using the brain of the creature mixed with water and spread out on the inside of the skin. I don't know if it will work. Just because something worked on Earth doesn't mean it will work here.

I have collected the material from the parachutes, the complete one from Transport Two and what little I can salvage from Transport One and have folded it up and stored it underneath the pinned down tanning skin. Once we get Transport Three safely landed, I'll move that material back inside.

We eat in silence. Lin is quiet. She has set up a bouncer for Hal who sits happily watching the toys suspended above him.

"Two more hours until Transport Three lands," I say just after taking my last bite of broccoli which I had steamed while grilling the meat.

Lin nods.

"We'll need to be outside when it lands."

Lin shakes her head. "It will be dark."

"You'll be with me, and I'll have the gun. The ships will be lit up. We'll be fine. We can't hide in here forever."

She looks at me, tears in her eyes. I put my hand on hers.

"It'll be fine," I say.

I jump up, kiss her, then kiss Hal, and grab a box of vegetables out of the fridge. I put the Glock on top and carry it out the door and past the tanning skins. After several trips, I have most of our essentials sitting a fair distance from the two transport ships. The plan is for Transport Three to land on the other side of the first one, close enough to form our three ship abode, so if there is a problem, the other two ships are more at risk than our position here several hundred yards away. I walk back to the ship as the sun sets. I know it's not THE sun, just a star over a million light years from Earth, but it's OUR sun now and for the rest of our lives.

I've been either so busy or so exhausted that I haven't

had the chance to really absorb being outside under a sky with horizons miles and miles away and not stuck in some tin can floating in space. The red and orange sky above the setting sun is breathtaking. The breeze is cooler than it has been all day and feels amazing on my bare skin.

I'm still carrying the Glock as I step up into the ship. I glance at the console screen and see that the countdown is under three minutes. Transport Three should be arriving about forty-five minutes after it launches out of the *Armstrong*.

"We should head outside," I say.

Lin nods, gets up from the dinner table where she has remained, takes Hal out of the bouncer, and carries him to the open hatch. I go down a couple of steps, the Glock in my right hand, turn and offer her my left. She glances out at the dark landscape, looks back at me, and takes it. We walk outside, the air refreshingly cool now that the sun is gone but not so cool that we are uncomfortable. The clouds arrived during the afternoon and moved on toward the horizon before sunset, so the sky above us is clear. As we walk, I look up to see several stars in the sky in an unfamiliar pattern. There is no Big Dipper or Little Dipper here. I try to spot one of the stars moving in relation to the others, but I don't look long enough to detect anything. The *Armstrong* should be visible from the planet surface, I think, so it should appear as one of those stars.

We walk through the tall grass to the spot where I stacked our supplies. It's dark enough that we can't see the spots where we are stepping. One of the things I want to do with the skin of that creature is make some kind of shoes or moccasins. If we are going to wear anything, it will be for protection, and our feet are the most vulnerable parts of our bodies while walking outside. I will also use the leather to make the belt with a holster for the Glock so I don't have to carry it in my hand all the time.

I set the Glock down on one of the boxes and offer to take Hal. Lin sighs as she hands him to me. He starts to fuss a little until I get him on my shoulder, upright so that he can look around. We see little flashes of lights between our spot and the jungle.

"What's that?" Lin asks.

"When I was growing up, we used to call them lightning bugs, but most people called them fireflies."

Lin looks at me then back at the lights. I realize I just referred to memories of Earth Kevin as my own, something I've been trying not to do.

"These may be different, of course," I say. "We are on another planet after all."

"They would be pretty if I wasn't so scared."

I start to tell her that there's nothing to be scared of, but I stop myself. It would be a lie, especially after the day we'd had. I think of the underground dwellers on one of the other continents on this planet, how we only ever saw them when the sun was down. They only came out to work their fields at night. Was that because it was more comfortable for them, living in the dark underground? Or was it because it was too dangerous for them to come out during the day? I suppose I'll never know now since I didn't choose that landing site.

I keep watching the sky, and I think I figure out which star is the one moving and, thus, the *Armstrong*. Transport 3 should have launched several minutes ago, during our walk over here. I doubt we'll see it directly above us until the chute deploys. Perhaps if we were further away, it might appear as a shooting star.

"That breeze feels nice," I say just to break the silence.

Lin had been staring out at the fireflies. She looks at me and Hal. "Yes."

"You have to admit these wide open spaces are a lot better than being stuck in a small space ship."

"It wasn't small." Lin points at the two transport craft. "Those are small."

"That's what I meant. We can't live our lives stuck in there. We have to get out and breathe the fresh air."

I expect her to say again that we should have stayed on the *Armstrong*, but she stays quiet, still looking at the fireflies or whatever they are. Part of me wants to go get a closer look, but I don't want to carry Hal over there. I also don't want to give him back to Lin. I cherish holding him every chance I get.

Movement in the sky catches my attention, and I look up, hoping to see a parachute. Instead, I see two of those blue creatures flying past. From the light of the two moons, I can see that they are still the same shade of blue as before. So they are only camouflaged during cloudless days. That's good to know. My free hand reaches for the Glock, but the bat-like creatures don't seem interested in us or in the remains of their friend. They seem to be flying with purpose toward a specific destination.

I relax when they get out of sight, leaving the Glock on the box. Hal tries to wiggle out of my arms, and I have to use both hands to keep him from falling.

"What are you doing?" I say to him.

Lin reaches for him, and I reluctantly hand him over. She puts him to her breast, and he immediately starts gobbling up whatever he can get. I move one of the sturdier boxes from the top of the stack down to the ground and motion for Lin to sit, which she does. After a few minutes I start pacing, not wanting to stay in the same spot but not wanting to leave Lin and Hal.

Transport 3 is almost here by the time I see it, underneath its red and white chute. Side thrusters move it laterally as it descends toward the other two transports. It comes down just on the other side of Transport One, its bottom engine firing to slow it down even more as it gently slides into place.

"Perfect landing," I say, smiling at Lin.

"Can we go inside now?" she asks.

"Yes."

I grab the box with the Glock on top of it and carry it back inside, following Lin. I don't want to leave anything outside, and by the time I'm done carrying everything in, I am exhausted. Lin and Hal are already asleep, and I fall into bed next to Lin and soon join them.

33

I wake up determined to make these three transport ships a comfortable home for Lin, Hal, and me. The ships are each a few inches apart from each other. I deploy wheels on Transport Two and pull it over to one until it bumps against it. After doing the same thing to the newly landed Transport Three, I go to work on the walls, removing them from the interior. Although they are designed for removal, it still takes a while as they also had to insulate passengers from the vacuum and cold of space. Once the walls are removed, I caulk the ceiling gaps. I finish this just in the nick of time as it begins raining outside as soon as I finish.

I stand in the open hatch watching and smelling the rain. It smells like a summer rain in South Dakota, and I can't stop the rush of memories that come flooding back. The one that takes precedence is sitting with Cynthia and Bobby on the bleachers at one of Thomas's high school baseball games, huddling under her tiny umbrella as the game inexplicably continues until, finally, the umpires signal for a delay with Thomas on deck. Here, there were still the smells of Earth, but there were no baseball fields, no high schools, no people.

I push the memories aside as I notice the rain hitting the stretched out skin of the dead creature. I run out into the rain, grab the folded up parachute material from under the skins and run it back inside. Dropping it on the floor near the hatch, I turn to start back and gasp. One of those giant blue bat things was standing just past the tanning skins, sniffing at the remains. The Glock is sitting nearby, but the thing is so far away that I think I'd have better aim with one of the rifles. I could take the Glock and run at it, but I don't remember how many rounds I have left in it. Like an idiot, I haven't reloaded it since yesterday. So I hurry to the weapons closet, taking one of the rifles and a box of ammo in a door beneath it and rush back, trying to load the rifle but dropping most of the cartridges to the floor as I go. When I get back to the hatch, still trying to load the rifle, the thing is gone. I set the rifle down, take the Glock, and walk down two steps, looking at the sky. I see the thing flying away, blue skin visible against the white clouds. The rain has stopped, so I decide to leave the skins where they are, now to dry.

I take the rifle, which is an AR-15 and has a magazine underneath the stock, and the Glock back to the weapons closet. I fully load the magazines of both and put the rifle back in its spot. I'll take it out later for some test shots like I had done with the Glock. Lin sits watching, so when I'm done, I take the Glock to her.

"This is a gun," I say. "Very powerful but very dangerous. We have it to keep us safe."

"I know. I've seen guns in movies."

I sometimes forget that while she has no memories of Earth, she has seen movies and television shows from the *Armstrong's* library. Hal begins crying from his spot in the bouncer, and Lin and I both get up and go to him, the Glock still in my hand.

"Later, when Hal is down for another nap, I want to give you a course in gun safety and shooting. But we can't shoot too much because we have a finite amount of ammunition."

Lin shrugs as she begins nursing Hal.

"In the meantime, don't touch it," I say.

She nods, and I get back to work setting up our house. Most of Transport 3 becomes our storage area. The bulk of our supplies are in what was Transport 3 anyway. I get the supplies we had brought with us on Transport 2 moved across to Three. Our bed in Transport 2 folds into the back wall as do the beds in the other two ships. We don't have to deploy those since it's just us, which gives us a lot of floor space. Each ship has a kitchen, but we are only using one of those. If an oven or fridge goes out, we can simply move one of the others over. Or, I suppose, switch kitchens.

We spend all day working to make our triple ship into a home, and we make a lot of progress by the time the sun begins setting in the west. During the day, I do check the console compartments to Transport 1 and Transport 3, but there is no Bible stored in either spot. How did Kacey's

Bible wind up in Transport 2? And what about the Kacey who lived out the rest of her days on Earth? Had she left the Bible on purpose, or had it been an accident? I remember her doing some simulator training during our time on the *Armstrong* in Earth orbit. Our *Armstrong* must have been that *Armstrong*. Now I can only wonder about the other five that Jordan talked about. Did they ever launch? During training, we only ever saw the one. I shake my head at Jordan and his mysteries. It's far too late to worry about them now.

I venture outside at dusk and pull up the stakes on the creature's hide. These skins are now dry and tanned. There is a distinctive odor, but it's not unpleasant. It's not quite the smell of leather that I remember from Earth either, but it will have to do. The membranes from the wings smell rotten, and I leave them outside on the ground. I drape the good skins over my shoulder and lug them back to the house.

I wake up the following morning to Hal's crying with a pulsing headache that only gets worse when I sit up. My head is so congested that I have to breathe through my mouth. I crawl over Lin who has a pillow over her head and stand up on shaky legs. Hal's face is red, snot running out of his nose and into his mouth. I wipe it off with my fingers. His face is hot to the touch. I pick him up and try to calm him on my shoulder. This usually works, but it doesn't this morning. He keeps wailing his angry cry.

"I know. I feel the same way," I tell him, and my voice sounds nasally.

Lin comes out from under her pillow, and she looks like

Hal and I feel. Her nose and cheeks are red. I put the back of my hand to her forehead, and she feels at least as hot as Hal.

"Looks like we are all sick," I say.

"Sick?"

"Yeah. We caught some kind of cold or flu virus or something."

Now that I think of it, we were never sick on the *Armstrong*. The air was all cycled through the ship after spending three billion years in the cold vacuum of space. There were no viruses to infect us. Our immune systems haven't had anything to do until now.

"I hate this," Lin says.

"Yeah, me too."

I sit on the edge of the bed.

"Here, take Hal. I'll see if I can find some antibiotics. If they even work."

Lin doesn't move, so I lay Hal in the space between her chest and her arm. She curls it around him. I get up and stagger to the storage area. I bypass the supplies we brought from the wheel section of the *Armstrong* and go straight to what had been stored on these transport ships. Unlike the wheel section, these have been in a weightless vacuum for the last twenty years while we were being grown and then living in that wheel section. So if the drugs retained their potency in that weightless vacuum, they should still be effective. I don't know what we'll do if they aren't effective.

I have to move three boxes to be able to get into the closet, but I find a supply of Z-packs. I grab two of them. Stopping in the kitchen, I retrieve two bottles of water and return to Lin. I open the first one and hand the first dose, two pills, to Lin.

"You have to swallow these whole, just like the Vitamin D pills on the *Armstrong*," I tell her.

I help her sit up and watch her take them one at a time. She falls back down, and I take my first two-pill dose.

"I don't know if these will work or not," I say. "Even if they're still effective, they may not work on whatever we have."

"I hate this place," Lin says. I don't have an argument to that at the moment.

I go back to the medicine closet to try to find something for Hal. The only thing I find that might help him is a bottle of liquid Tamiflu. Hal makes a terrible face when I give him a dose, but he manages to swallow it between wails. I move him to Lin's other side, crawl over both of them, lying down with Hal between us so he won't roll off the bed.

I spend the rest of the day in and out of sleep. I awaken whenever Hal cries. Lin, in a daze of her own, tries breast feeding him, but he rejects this. Her milk must be overheated from her fever. And when it hits Hal's stomach, his own fever will probably heat it more. I wonder if I can give him cooler milk in a bottle.

I crawl over the two of them, thinking I should move the bed away from the wall so I can get up without having to crawl over them but not having the energy to do it right now. I pull some of the milk that Lin pumped before we left the *Armstrong* out of the fridge, put it in a baby bottle and heat it up in a bottle warmer to just over 90 degrees Fahrenheit. I pick Hal up and bring him into another room, wanting to let Lin rest. I sit in the same chair I occupied for our entry into the planet's atmosphere and feed him the bottle. I sigh with relief as he seems to take to it.

My headache is worse than ever, and I find myself nodding off as I feed the baby. I'm afraid of dropping him to the floor, so I force myself to stay awake, wiping my runny nose on my free forearm.

"I don't guess you've ever read *War of the Worlds* by H. G. Wells, have you?" I say to Hal.

His eyes are closed as he ignores me and slowly sucks down the contents of the bottle. But I have to keep myself awake, so I keep talking.

"So, in the book, these advanced Martians come and attack Earth, and we humans have very feeble defenses. The Martians are on the verge of taking over everything when they all start dying. Why? Because of a virus. They all got sick, and the Earth was saved. I think that's what's happening here, except in reverse. We were all set to start a new human civilization here. We came over a million light years, and now, every human on the planet is sick and wants to die."

Hal's sucking slows and stops as I talk. When I'm sure he's asleep, I pull the bottle away, the nipple making a small pop when it leaves his mouth. He radiates heat as he snuggles against my chest in my arm. I should get up, put the bottle in the fridge and get back in bed. But I am having trouble finding the energy to do any of that.

34

The light coming in from the window dims as the sun goes down. I have tilted the chair back, and Hal sleeps on my chest. I am in and out, dozing but opening my eyes every so often whenever Hal shifts or a noise from outside filters in. The console in front of me flashes a low battery warning, and I remember that I haven't deployed the solar panels yet. I haven't removed the chute from the top of Transport 3 yet. I wonder if I could have the AI deploy the panel just on Transport 2. The wind has been blowing the chutes the other direction. But then I wonder, *what's the point?* What are the chances that any of us will survive this virus given the state of our immune systems? If either Lin or I die, the whole thing is over. But I stop and think. No, Lin is the only indispensable person here.

If either Hal or I die, the other of us could still father more children with Lin. I find that distasteful, but it's true. We could resort to incest to keep the human race from dying out. We are already going to have to resort to that among siblings.

But if Lin dies, it's all over. No more humans. Hal and I would be it. The end.

Hal stirs, and I realize I've been mumbling my thoughts.

"Sorry buddy," I whisper.

I grab the half full bottle, wondering how long it has been sitting out, stumble to the kitchen, and put it in the fridge. I manage to not drop Hal which seems miraculous considering how I feel and how much he's sliding around in my arms because of all the sweat we've generated. Lin is sleeping, but she still feels like a furnace is burning inside her. I should get a thermometer and see how dangerously high her fever is getting, but I don't have the energy. I probably don't want to know anyway and needlessly alarm myself. I crawl over Lin, placing Hal between us, and lie down.

It's still dark the next time I wake up. Hal is fussing but hasn't gone into a full cry. I worry that he might be too weak to fully cry. Lin rolls out of bed. I hear her pee. When she comes back, she tries to get Hal to nurse, but he refuses and falls back into a fitful sleep.

It's daylight and hot in our room when I wake up again. The power has shut itself off. I roll over Hal and Lin and stagger to the console. I try to tell myself that I am feeling a little better, but I know I would be lying. My head feels like it could explode any minute, and part of me wishes it would just hurry up and do it. I haven't eaten in a day, but the thought of food makes me want to throw up. I flip a switch to run on emergency reserve power.

"Alexis, deploy solar panel on Transport Two," I say when the console finishes booting.

I hear the apparatus above me unfolding itself and say a prayer of thanks. At least we won't die from a lack of air conditioning. I grab two more bottles of water. Lin and I have been staying hydrated whenever we wake up. When I get back to the bedroom, I take my second dose from the Z-pack, although I doubt that it's doing any good, and wake Lin up to take hers. Maybe I'm imagining it, but she doesn't feel as hot as she did last night. I climb back over Hal and Lin and lie back down, exhausted from what little I did.

It is still daylight the next time I wake up, but the shadows are longer. It must be late afternoon or evening. I reach over, but Lin and Hal are gone.

"Lin?" I call.

I think to myself that I should get up, but it takes me a few minutes to muster the energy to do so. When I do stand up, I'm so dizzy that I almost fall down. My head still hurts, but it's more of a pressure headache now, from my clogged up sinuses. I find Lin in the seat where I had fed Hal several hours ago. She looks at me. Her cheeks don't look as flushed as they had earlier.

"Are you feeling better?" I ask.

"I don't know."

I sit down in the chair next to her, the one she had sat in during our trip to the planet surface. Hal is nursing almost frantically.

"He doesn't think your milk is too hot anymore," I say as I place the back of my hand on Lin's forehead. She doesn't even feel warm anymore.

The way my head feels, I'm sure I still have a fever. But somehow, it doesn't seem as bad as it has been.

"Maybe we'll survive this thing."

Lin nods. "I don't want to die anymore."

"Did you before?"

"Yes. It was awful. I don't want to be sick like that ever again."

"Hopefully our antibodies will build up and be able to fight off any more viruses."

"There are more of them?"

"Sure. This is a whole new ecosystem. We have been living in an artificial, controlled environment. People weren't meant to live that way, which is why I wanted to get us down here."

"You mean, we're supposed to be sick?"

"It's a natural part of life. We get infected; our bodies fight it off."

"That's stupid."

I start to argue, once again, for the merits of living on the planet rather than on the *Armstrong*, but I don't have the energy. So I just sit quietly looking out the window toward the setting sun. Part of me agrees with some of her sentiments though. Is this all there is, living alone and fighting for survival on a hostile planet? The Earth was, of course, hostile too, but we overcame it and built a civilization. Could we manage to increase our numbers enough to start our own civilization before we all die off? This train of thought is depressing, so I turn to something else.

"We should eat something," I say, slapping my thighs and getting up to find the chicken soup mix.

"I don't feel hungry," Lin says.

"We should eat something anyway."

It takes two more days before any of us is feeling anything close to well. Lin and Hal seem to fare better than I do as I just can't get rid of the lethargy. I spend the next two days in bed while Lin spends her time arranging the layout of our three-ship house. When I emerge, she has pulled up the two chairs and assembled the leather sofa that used to be under the console and arranged them around the large view screen on the back wall.

"Wow," I say. "Looks like a regular living room."

"You like it?"

"Yeah."

My head is still aching, so I take a couple of the Tylenol pills. Hal's bouncer is in front of the screen facing us, and he sits happily swatting the toys on the mobile above him.

"Hey there, little guy," I say, bending over. "You look like you feel a lot better."

He looks at me and smiles, and my heart melts. Lin has turned her attention to whatever it is she's cooking. The way she has arranged it makes it look like one of those houses with an open floor plan, the living spaces all visible to each other. I walk up behind her and put my arms around her waist.

"I think I'm pregnant," she says.

It takes a moment for me to comprehend the words.

"That's wonderful," I say and caress her belly. "I thought it had been a while since your last period."

It's funny how living without clothes like we are makes things like that general knowledge. We have no secrets.

Since childbearing and childrearing were the main functions at this stage of our mission, each transport ship was supplied with ultrasound machines and a lot of the things we would need for a safe delivery. I tell myself that I have to stop thinking of this as a mission. We have no one to report back to, no one to assess any success or failure. We are here, and this is life. It's not a mission anymore. But if we want humanity to continue, we have to have as many babies as possible, even though we open ourselves to danger and heartbreak.

I kiss Lin's neck as she stirs the soup she's making. My stomach rumbles as the aroma from the pot reaches my nostrils, and for the first time in several days, I feel almost all right.

35

I still tire easily for the next few days, and I stay mainly indoors working with the newly created leather from the skin of that flying monster. I make myself a belt. Thankfully, there is a plastic holster in the weapons closet that the Glock fits into, and I loop that into the belt. I don't have anything to make a decent buckle, so I make some extra slack so that I can just tie it around my waist. I then cut part of the rest of the leather into strips and small threads and use those to make Lin a pair of moccasins. I'm not very efficient and wind up wasting a lot of it. I have just enough left to make moccasins for myself. I will keep the scraps for future projects, assuming, of course, I kill another one of those things or some other animal.

My first excursion out of our little house in almost a week is to the site of the landing probe and its broken solar panel. I'm outfitted with my moccasins, the belt with the holstered Glock on my right hip, a bottle of water, and the AR-15 rifle, fully loaded this time. I invite Lin to come with me, but she decides she'd rather stay inside than have to carry Hal all that way. I don't blame her for that.

I go in the late afternoon. The stairs retract and the hatch closes almost as soon as I hit the ground. I look back and see Lin's face through the window on the door. We wave at each other, and I turn and start walking. The sky is overcast, which is good since it will make those flying things easier to spot. It rained for a couple of hours earlier in the afternoon. I still watch every spot where I step. The moccasin soles are not so thick that I feel confident in them. Lander 15 is only about six feet tall without the solar panel on top. The drone sits in its spot near the top, unused for the last several years. The solar panel is on the ground next to it, most of the glass cells shattered into tiny fragments. Those fragments look sharp, so I avoid them as I step around the area. The arm of the solar panel is broken at the base, almost as if the panel was too heavy for it.

I circle the landing probe, but nothing else appears damaged. As I am about to lean forward and remove the drone from its bay, I happen to glance over at our house and see two of the blue bat things on the roof. They are watching me silently. Leaving the drone where it is, I begin stalking back to the house. I realize that I've never test fired the rifle, having been sick for the past week. I stop about three hundred feet from the house, raise the rifle, and take aim at one of the creatures.

"Get off my house," I say and pull the trigger.

I must have missed high as I don't hear anything strike the house. The two creatures immediately take flight toward me. I shoot again, hitting one of them. It falls toward me as the other one veers off to the left. I shoot the falling creature again, thinking that if it hits me, I want to make sure it's dead. It crashes to the ground about twenty feet in front of me, rolling and stopping just in front of my feet. That second shot took almost half its head off, so I'm sure enough that it's dead that I point the rifle toward its companion. The thing is flying away from me. I start to pull the trigger, but I stop, thinking that I should conserve my ammo. I point the gun back at the downed creature. It spasms and stops moving. At least I'll be able to make some more of the leather, and we'll have more meat. It's a good thing we have three refrigerator freezers in our three-ship house.

Not expecting to have to butcher another creature, I didn't bring a knife with me, so I stalk back to get one. I'm thinking that two or more of those things must have perched on Lander 15's solar panel until it gave way. That's the best explanation. There's so much I don't know about those things. Where do they live when they aren't flying? How far can they fly? Are they able to cross the oceans and go to the other continents? Do they have any predators of their own, or are they the apex of this planet? In all my time on the *Armstrong* looking at video, I never saw anything that would seem able to challenge them.

"Well, *we* are here now," I say out loud, although I silently wonder how dominant we can be once our Earth-made ammunition runs out.

I spend the next day tanning the skin of the second creature with the portion of its brain that I can salvage after that shot to the head, and Lin and I eat another meal with steaks from this new kill. I no longer trust the meat from that first one since we lost power to the refrigerators while we were sick. I throw all that out, carrying it back over to the site of the landing probe, and restock the fridges with this new one.

"I'm going to go check out the river tomorrow morning," I say during dinner.

Lin looks at me. "What river?"

"The one that runs through the middle of the jungle."

She frowns and looks back down at her plate.

"I'll have two guns and a machete," I say. "I'll be careful. But I want to see if that's a viable water supply. We'll need water for growing crops if we don't for some reason get enough rain."

"What do I do if you don't come back?"

"Why wouldn't I come back?"

She gives me a look that seems to say, "Are you serious?"

"We have radios. I used to call them walkie-talkies when I was a kid. I'll carry one with me and show you how to use one of the other ones. So we can talk with each other. I think the range on these is at least five miles." *If they work at all*, I think, but I don't say out loud.

I will also need to figure out how to hang the radio to my belt, or cut myself a second belt from the new hide. Lin takes another bite of her steak and doesn't look at me.

Sighing, I get up and head to the weapons closet where I find four walkie-talkies. They are plugged into wall sockets, getting a charge from the house's battery which has now been charged by the solar panels. I take two of them, power them on, and set them to the same channel, thinking that it doesn't matter here which channel I choose. The feedback I get when they are next to each other indicates that they work.

I take them to Lin and show her how to listen and talk on them. I put it on my belt with the Glock in its holster and create a loop with one of the scraps so that a radio can hang off my other hip.

"It's a little heavy, but it's workable," I say to Lin when I stand in front of her with it on.

She just shakes her head, reaches out and grabs my penis, which is her not-so-subtle way of saying she wants sex. Hal is asleep in the bouncer, so I take off the belt and comply.

36

It is still dark when I step outside. I woke Lin to tell her
I was going and to leave the radio with her. She set that
radio on my pillow and appeared to go back to sleep. I let
her. Hal will wake her up soon anyway. I am wearing the
moccasins and the belt with the Glock and radio attached
to it, the blue of the leather now fading to gray. I found
an old leather strap for the rifle, and I have it slung over
one shoulder along with a pouch which holds a bottle of
water and an empty bottle to use if I can get close enough
to the river to get a sample. In my right hand is a machete
for hacking through the jungle, although I could use it as
a weapon as well.

I think that it ought to feel strange to be so equipped
while also still naked, but it feels rather normal. Lin and

I have been naked since we woke up over a year ago, so we've gotten used to it. Even if we had clothes, I'm pretty sure Lin would refuse to wear them.

When I do step outside I consider going back in to get a flashlight. There is only one moon visible in the sky, but it's probably the one that's farthest away and is only half full and obscured by passing clouds. But I'm already weighed down by everything I'm carrying, and there is a slight glow on the horizon to the east. It will be light enough to see by the time I reach the edge of the jungle, so I walk that direction. My eyes keep turning toward the sky. I can't get the image of those flying monsters out of my mind. I keep listening for that sound of flapping wings that I heard the day before when the two creatures took off from the roof of our house. Except for the sounds of my footfalls in the grass, everything is deathly quiet. That begins to change the closer I get to the edge of the jungle canopy. Most of the sounds I hear from there sound like insect noises, like cicadas but different enough to sound alien to me.

I reach the edge of the trees just as the first hint of the sun emerges on the horizon. It is now light enough to see clearly. There are clouds above, so I scan the sky but see no sign of the blue flying monsters. I should name them something. In the Bible, God left it to Adam to name all the beasts, so I suppose on this planet, that responsibility should fall to me. With everything we have to do to set ourselves up to survive here, naming things seems trivial. The sounds of the jungle are loud and varied now but nothing that seems threatening, no wildcat roars or anything, although I can't forget the green feline-looking animal from the video taken by the landing probe that sits less than a mile from here. The brush is thick, and I cut a path through it with the machete, making enough noise to scare any animals away.

Once I'm in among the taller trees, the brush on the ground is more sparse, probably due to a lack of sunlight hitting the ground. It seems more like a forest than a jungle. The trees tower above everything creating a deep shade that limits visibility this early in the morning. Various small insects flitter around my face, and I wave them away with my free hand. After walking a few hundred yards, I stop, trying to find the light in the sky so I know how to keep going in the same direction but unable to because of the dense foliage above. I haven't had to use the machete in a while, and as I glance around, I see that I am on a game trail of some kind. So I continue in the same direction, hoping I can use the same trail to get me back.

When the radio squawks, I pull it out and say, "Lin, it's me. I'm in the forest, over."

"Are you OK?"

I wait for her to say "over" like I taught her, but she doesn't.

"I'm fine. I'm still not to the river yet. Over."

"Okay. Hal is up, and I am feeding him."

I wait another few seconds, roll my eyes, and say, "Lin, you have to say 'over' so I know when you've stopped talking because we can't both talk at the same time. Over."

"Oh, I forgot. Um, over. That sounds dumb."

"Fine. Whatever. I'll call if I see anything unusual. Over and out."

I put the radio back into the loop on my belt and ignore

her telling me to be careful. The game trail turns when it hits more heavy brush. I hack away at that, thinking that I hear water beyond, but it only leads into more heavy brush. The animals have to have water though, so I back up and follow the game trail when it turns alongside the vegetation. No longer knowing which direction I'm going, I follow the winding trail through a break in the brush and finally see the river. The bed is wide to accommodate heavy flooding, either from rainstorms or from the occasional extreme tides when the three moons get together and create havoc in certain parts of the planet. I climb down a rocky embankment to get to the soft sand and approach the river. The water is flowing at a leisurely pace about three hundred or so yards wide, reminding me of the river that runs through one of my favorite towns, Missoula, Montana. I push the thought away, not wanting to sadden myself over things that are long gone.

Something large slides by out in the middle of the water, either a really big fish or a long snake, although it could be something else entirely. I need to stop comparing what I see here to things on Earth. The Glock is in my hand before I realize I've pulled it out of the holster. The thing in the river swims upstream, ignoring me as I stand at the foot of the rocks far from the water's edge. Once it passes, I creep forward, holstering the Glock and pulling the empty clear plastic water bottle from my pouch. After unscrewing the lid, I crouch down and put the bottle in the water, looking all around as it fills. When done, I screw the lid back on and look at it, seeing several tiny swimming things in the light brown water.

I slip the bottle back into my bag, pull out the other one

that I filled with fresh water last night and take a long drink. I see a few fish-like creatures swim by in the shallow part of the river near where I'm standing, and I wonder if I can rig a trip to catch some of them. Will they taste like fish on earth? It will be interesting to find out.

As I stand looking around, the edge of the water encroaches on me, quickly soaking my moccasins, and I scramble back to the embankment and start climbing the rocks. When I get back to the top, I look down and see that the water level hasn't made it to the base. Just knowing I'm on a planet with three moons and seeing video of a rapid tidal flood, I don't want to ever take my chances with any body of water.

The sun is high enough now that the light reflects off the top of the water, but I can still see a variety of moving things below the surface. The river is teeming with life, a potential source of food for a long time to come. I start to turn away, to head back up the trail, when I see one of those green catlike creatures on the other side of the river. It stops and looks at me, its ears larger than that of an Earth feline, the face more streamlined with no whiskers. It seems to be the same species as the creature I saw on the video taken years ago by the probe lander. It's so far away that I have difficulty determining its exact size, but it looks about as large as a bobcat. It sits on its haunches and lets out a long high-pitched roar. Two more of the the things appear on my side of the river about a hundred yards downstream. They look at their fellow feline across the river and then at me. I set the machete down and take the rifle in both hands, pointed toward them.

"You don't want any of this," I say.

The two green felines let out roars identical to the one

across the river. I fire a warning shot over their heads, and they shut up and scramble back into the brush. The shot probably scares off any animal that might have been lurking around. I put the rifle back on my shoulder hanging by its strap and pick up the machete. I walk along the top of the rocks in the opposite direction from where the felines had been. I see tracks shaped roughly like triangles in the mud down along the edge of the water. They look like deer tracks. A supply of venison would be wonderful. The tracks follow the edge of the water for a few yards and then disappear at the bottom of the rocks. Whatever the animal is, it had come up here and gone through the opening in the brush. I follow the trail, but I stop when I see another of the prints.

"Okay, so it's a small deer," I say in a whisper.

When I finally get a glimpse of the animal on the trail ahead of me, it looks more like a long-legged badger, with gray fur. It has four legs, each of which is about the height of my waist kind of like a deer, but those legs are so close together because of the small body, it just seems like they would bang into each other if the thing were to try to run at top speed. Its body seems plump, like a fat rabbit or something. It would probably make a good meal, especially the muscles of the upper rear legs, but I don't want to just start killing things right away. I watch it move through the forest for a few minutes, staying just far enough back to see it. It stops near one of the bushes and eats a few berries from it. The bushes are tall, which makes the long legs convenient. Two more of the long-legged things emerge from the bushes next to the first. One of them looks at me and freezes. The other two turn and look right at me as well. I pull the Glock from the holster just in case they charge at me, but they all turn and run off into the bushes. I hurry over and find the gap where they disappeared, but I decide not to follow. I'm already further off the trail than I intended.

I follow my own tracks back to the spot where I had spotted the felines and find the path I had used to get to the river. Feeling not so lost now, I crouch, not wanting to put my bare butt on the ground with all the leaves and brambles, and watch the river flow. That makes me think of an old Bob Dylan song that I hadn't heard in years even before the training for this mission. I wonder if it is in the database of our transport ship. It seems to have been one of his lesser known songs. I'll have to check when I get back.

Across the river, a black creature that looks like a cross between a miniature bear and a moose, with big paws and antlers jutting out from the sides if its head that look like paddle boards, bounds into the water. It swipes one of those paws and comes up with a fish. From here, it looks like a normal trout from Earth. The moose-bear puts the fish in its mouth and bounds back up the bank and back into the forest.

In just a few minutes, I have encountered felines, long legged badgers, a giant river creature, and a bear-moose thing. I remember hiking in Glacier National Park and seeing fewer animals than that in an entire day. This forest is filled with life, taking advantage of the water of the river and the cover of the trees from the flying blue monsters. I have seen and learned more than I planned on for this first excursion here.

Turning away from the river, I almost step on a dark gray creature about the size of a gerbil. It waddles away down the rock embankment toward the river. It looks kind of like a gerbil too, but it appears to have six legs. Shaking my head, I start back up the trail, making each step deliberate. The animals here aren't used to seeing hunters or humans of any kind, so I have to be ready for anything. I use the path through the brush I had cut earlier and emerge at the edge of the grassy field. On top of our house is another one of those flying blue monsters.

I stop, scanning the sky for any movement. The clouds have either burnt off or moved on, so there is a lot of blue above. I look back at the thing on my roof. It is watching me, and I can only wonder if it's the one that had gotten away yesterday. I have the AR-15 and the Glock with me, but I also have the machete. I swing it around a bit, letting the thing watch me, and take a few steps out into the field. The thing on the house doesn't move. I look up in the sky, but I don't see any movement.

"I've killed two of you bastards," I say out loud. "I bet you're not used to being the hunted, are you?"

The thing on the house lifts up, spreading its wings, but it remains on the roof. I hold the machete up and swing it across in front of me.

"Fuck you," I say to the thing on the roof.

It pushes off and flies straight toward me, it's mouth open in an evil looking grin. I stand with my legs apart, raise the machete up like it's a baseball bat and I'm about to try to hit one into left field. I swing just as the thing is about to hit me. It pulls up, and the point of the machete slices through the main body of the thing. Blood sprays onto me as it flies over me and then crashes to the ground and bounces into the edge of the brush from which I had just emerged. I run toward it as it tries to right itself, smashing the blade across the top of its head just before it takes to the air, pulling the handle of the machete out of my hand. It flies a little way toward the house as I pull the Glock from its holster. Before I can take aim at the thing, it crashes to the ground, shudders once, and lies still. I walk slowly toward it, ignoring the squawking of the radio and Lin's voice calling my name, glancing up at the sky with every step. When I reach the creature, I grab the handle of the machete with my free hand and pull it free from the thing's head. I consider putting a bullet in that head, just to make sure it's dead, but I decide to conserve my ammo. Besides, the machete had been buried so deep that it had to have hit brain tissue and killed the thing. I grab the end of one wing and try dragging the carcass so that it is under the house, but it's so heavy that the wing begins to rip before I can get very far.

I think I see something moving in the sky above, so I drop the wing and sprint to the house.

"Alexis, open the port door on Transport Two," I say in a loud voice when I get close.

The stairs deploy as the door slides open. I bound up the steps, stopping at the top one to look at the sky. I don't see anything moving. The blue creature still lies in a heap where I had left it. Lin runs over to the open hatch and pulls me inside before I can confirm whether there is another one of those things in the sky or not.

"I'm all right," I say amidst her clutching at me.

She grabs my face and turns me toward her even as I'm still looking for more of those blue creatures and looks me right in the eyes.

"I'm fine."

"I was scared."

I turn my full attention to her. "I know. I'm sorry."

She kisses me, grabs my shoulders and pushes me back, looking me up and down. She stops at my thigh, rubbing a spot that now stings. I look down and see the red spot.

"A bug bite," I say.

I think nothing of it. Mosquito bites are common anywhere I — or Earth Kevin — ever lived. Lin does a full circle around me as I tell the AI to close the door. She finds four more bites, all on my legs.

"Chiggers," I say, remembering the term we used when I was a kid.

"Sit," Lin orders, motioning to one of the old cockpit chairs.

I smile and sit as she grabs a first aid kid and swabs at the bites with alcohol pads.

"I didn't even feel them bite me," I say, but Lin is not to be deterred. She has watched all of the first aid training videos, after all.

"There," she says when she's done and kisses me on the mouth.

37

I test the water sample I took from the river. The computer analyzes sixty-four different species of animals, plants, and bacteria, only six of which are close to anything on Earth.

"So we'd have to boil any water from the river before drinking it," I tell Lin. "But it would be that way most places on Earth too."

My plan is to go out at dusk and butcher this latest kill, but the things that bit me are apparently more potent than chiggers or North American mosquitos. Each bite swells into a large red whelp that looks like a marble has been inserted under my skin. To make matters worse, my head congestion and fever return. I lie down after a lunch of creature meat and Brussel sprouts.

"Alexis, play 'Watching the River Flow' by Bob Dylan," I say.

"'Watching the River Flow' by Bob Dylan is not in the database. Songs by Bob Dylan include 'All Along the Watchtower', 'Knocking on Heaven's Door', 'Like a Rolling Stone', 'The Times They Are'—"

"Alexis, never mind," I say, cutting her off.

I close my eyes and drift off, and I don't awaken until the following morning, feeling much worse.

Lin and Hal seem fine, and I reluctantly tell Lin to keep the baby away from me just in case I'm contagious. I get up at one point to look out the windows, checking the area outside. The dead creature is still where it fell, but I don't see any others. I fly the drone from Transport Two around the area, mainly to make sure there aren't any more on top of the house since they seem to like to perch there. But the house is clear. I figure that it's too late to salvage either the meat or the hide from the latest kill, so I begin another Z-pack antibiotic treatment and go to bed over in Transport Three, as far from Lin and Hal as I can get.

The red welts go away before the fever and cold symptoms do, which tells me that they are unrelated. Two days after killing that third blue creature, I am feeling better. I don't know if it's because of the Z-pack or because I've built up antibodies to fight the infections on this planet, but I finish the taking the Z-pack over the next couple of days anyway.

At dusk, about twelve hours after my fever breaks, I walk toward the forest, armed with both the Glock and the AR-15. The stench of the dead creature hits me when I get within ten yards of it, so I turn around and head back. I didn't bring the machete with me, so I couldn't hack another path through the brush, not that I wanted to with darkness falling. I stop after a few steps, just looking at our homestead, plotting where a garden will go. We have seeds from the hydroponic garden on the *Armstrong*. It's time to see if the minerals in this soil will support plants from Earth. We have to start growing our own food. If we have to, we can tend the garden at night, like the humanoid creatures I observed on that other continent. Whether they did it because of the threat of the flying creatures, sensitivity to sunlight, or to avoid the heat of the day is still up for speculation. It doesn't matter to us now. Lin and I will do what we have to do.

Work on the garden starts the following morning. Jordan supplied each transport ship with a plethora of gardening tools, knowing that we would likely have to raise our own food. I saw a variety of plant life on my excursion to the forest but nothing that bore an obvious fruit or vegetable. Of course, I didn't dig anything up to check the roots, looking for this planet's equivalent to carrots, potatoes, radishes, or any other root-based vegetable.

I get up before dawn and grab the tiller from Transport 3. Wearing the belt with the holstered Glock on it, my moccasins, and nothing else, I cut a square on the east side of our house about twenty feet to each side, then work toward the middle, removing the grass that is dug up and piling it up under our house. The soil looks good. I only have to remove seven rocks from the tilled area. I stop just as the sun is fully above the horizon and head inside, tucking the tiller under the house with the discarded grass. Lin is awake and feeding Hal when I walk in.

"You know what I wish we had?" I say.

"What?"

"Eggs. Real eggs. But I haven't seen any birds on this planet. Just those flying monstrosities, and who knows how or where they reproduce."

We are low on 3-D printed bacon, but I fry some of what's left anyway along with the fake scrambled eggs from the *Armstrong*.

"Biscuits would be good too," I say, more talking to myself now. "But we need flour. And for flour, we need wheat or some other kind of grain. I wonder if we could find something like that growing naturally around here. I mean, we have a huge field of tall grass, but there's no grain on them. We can grow corn. I guess we could make cornbread biscuits."

I notice Lin just staring at me.

"Sorry," I say.

She shrugs. "We just need food."

"I know. I'm talking out loud. This isn't Earth, so some things will be different. Maybe we'll find something better than biscuits one day."

"Maybe."

I serve our plates and sit down across from Lin.

"When I signed up for this mission, I thought I would just be pretending to be an astronaut for a few weeks. We'd go through training and then go on with our lives. And we did. I did. And yet, I'm here now too. I never gave a moment's thought as to how difficult it would be to live on another planet with different flora and fauna. We've only been here a few days, and we've all been sick. I've been sick twice. I've been attacked and had to kill three of those unimaginable things. I'm still having trouble believing any of this is real, you know."

Lin looks away from me and over at Hal. "I'm real. He's real. That should be enough."

"You are. I'm just venting. We'll make this work."

"I wish we'd stayed on the ship. You wish you were still Earth Kevin. But here we are. With Hal. We have to make this place livable for him and for us."

She looks back at me, and I nod my head.

"You're right," I say. "You're absolutely right. I need to stop thinking about what we don't have and concentrate on what we do have or what we can grow or make."

I reach across the table and take her hand.

"Thank you."

She smiles and nods.

<h1 style="text-align:center">38</h1>

The next morning, I plant almost half of our seed supply, hoping that anything will grow in this alien soil. The lack of a significant planetary axis tilt means there are no discernible seasons. We are fairly near the equator anyway, so even if there were, we wouldn't experience much difference. But it does rain more often the week after planting the seeds than it did the previous weeks since our arrival. Having seen no more of the flying blue creatures, I climb out and onto the roof and rig up a rain collection system using the remains of the parachutes. Over the next few days, our water tanks are almost completely refilled.

Unfortunately, our waste tanks are filling fast as well, and we don't have the option of emptying them into space. I have enough pipe to make a sewer line out almost a hundred yards. I pick a direction toward more open field, thinking that it's slightly downhill and that we just don't go that way very often, and, at dusk one night, head out and dig a hole as deep as I can get it, which is about ten feet before I hit bedrock or something. I run the piping out to the hole by moonlight and then open the tanks so that it drains into the hole.

I sleep a few hours after building our makeshift sewer system before getting up and stepping outside, finding that several of the planted vegetables have sprouted and broken through the surface. I only have to water the garden twice over the next few days as the rain is plentiful. We have enough drinking and bathing water that I don't have to retrieve any water from the river.

I do make a few early morning excursions to the forest, sighting several more animals. I pick up more insect bites each time I go. They swell as before, but I don't experience the fever or congestion like I did after that first excursion. Something that looks like a deer but smaller and gray with white stripes surprises me in the forest on my fifth excursion, and I wind up shooting it with the Glock. It bounds off into the brush and collapses. I shoot it in the head to end its suffering and put it on my back. Carrying it back to the house takes longer than I expect. It's cloudy, so I'm able to spot one of those blue creatures flying toward me. Dropping my load, I pull the Glock and fire at its head. Its scream seems to pierce my eardrum as it flies over me and crashes directly into the trees, not able to lift up and over them. I consider going back into the forest after it, but I decide to carry on with my original load.

I have trouble getting the miniature deer thing back on my shoulders and wind up dragging it the rest of the way to the house. I butcher it under Transport Two, stretching the hide with a mixture made from its brain like I had done with the first two creatures I had killed and taking the meat inside. Most of it goes in the freezer, but I grill some of it for dinner that night. It is the best tasting meal we've had since waking up on the *Armstrong*. Lin loves it.

The garden makes steady progress. In a few weeks, we have quite a supply of corn and cucumbers. I try my hand at grinding some of the corn to make meal and then cornbread. It turns out all right, but I miss having butter with it. But I don't complain to Lin. We concentrate on what we have, not what we don't have.

I am able to coax Lin out of the house a few times late in the evening. She enjoys feeling the breeze in her hair. Hal smiles and laughs when we hold him waist high and let him feel the tops of the grass. We gradually begin going outside earlier as we never see any of the flying monstrosities anymore, although I do carry both the Glock and the rifle every time we do go out. Did I kill all of the monsters in this vicinity, or did the others communicate after losing four of their number near our house, warning them not to fly over us? We begin seeing forest animals venturing out into the grassy area earlier in the day. One evening, I watch fourteen of the miniature deer run outside the brush. That first one tasted so good that I grab the rifle to try to bag one of these, but they are gone before I can look into the gun's scope.

For the first time since we've been here, I can see all three moons in the sky. The one that appears the largest is directly overhead, while the other two are closer to the horizon. The one overhead is full. One of the others is a crescent, and the other is at the half stage. I have to fight an impulse to go to the river and see how much water is flowing now. There is enough light to see even long after the sun is set, but I don't want to leave Lin and Hal. And just because all three are visible at the same time doesn't necessarily mean that they are creating one of those super high tides. I chose this land locked site so I wouldn't have to worry about those.

We watch the full moon for a few minutes. This one is brown, the light reflecting from the sun makes it appear amber from here. The half moon is the one that looks most like the moon of earth, gray and pockmarked with craters. The moon that is currently a crescent is covered with water and has a small nitrogen-based atmosphere. It contains a bit of oxygen; how could it not with such an abundance of water, but not enough to sustain human life. Of course, it is always freezing there, so its color is a smooth whitish blue. Still, there could be life under the surface if the core of that moon is able to warm the water enough.

"We were all so disappointed that there was never any life in our solar system, other than on Earth," I say.

"What?" Lin asks.

"Nothing. Just thinking out loud."

We walk back up the steps and inside without another word, as if we just both decided at the same time to go in.

The garden thrives, and we soon have a plethora of vegetables to eat. I continue to use the guns to hunt game, particularly those miniature gray and white deer, but I feel a bit guilty with each round of ammunition expended. I set about making a primitive bow and a few arrows out of whatever I can find around our site. In the forest I find a branch to make the bow, and some of the meat from one of those flying monsters provides a string of sinew long enough to complete it. It's the arrows that are the trouble. I find enough sticks straight enough to create arrows along with some rocks that I am able to carve into points. When I try to take my first test shots, the arrows fly in all directions except for the one I'm aiming at. They also don't travel far before the weight of the arrowhead drops them to the ground.

I experiment with different things on the arrows, but with a lack of birds here, there is also a lack of feathers. I have trouble finding anything light enough but also strong enough to serve as the fletching on the backs of the arrows. Everything I try for an arrowhead is heavy, so I take to sharpening the ends of the arrow sticks themselves.

While I struggle creating the archery tools, I am able to make a trap that works at catching those miniature deer. After setting it near the spot where I first killed one of those deer, I check the trap every day. On the third, I am rewarded with our first meat not killed with a bullet from Earth. Our freezers are beginning to fill up with meat, so I try making jerky out of some of the excess. I can do it in the oven, but I want to plan on a contingency where we don't have any power. I build a rack to hold the meat slices as they dry in the sun, but less than an hour after putting it out, that meat is gone, picked off by one of those flying monsters.

Our sightings of those creatures diminishes after killing

that fourth one though. Yes, I lose the jerky, but I hadn't put much of it out. The next time I try making jerky, I dehydrate it in the oven. Lin and I have trouble chewing and swallowing what results. We both decide we should stick to freezing our excess meat for now.

Lin's pregnancy progresses, and Hal grows at a fast pace. Every little milestone, his first time crawling, his first tooth, his first time pulling himself to a standing position, reminds me of the three kids Earth Kevin had. I am careful not to say anything around Lin. She seems to take offense to anything I mention related to Earth even though she's watched so many movies and TV shows from there.

During a routine ultrasound check, Lin and I are shocked to discover twins.

"That's good," I say. "We need to produce a lot of children, and we can have more of them if they come two at a time."

I don't tell her about the twins one of Earth Kevin's cousins had prematurely. They came out weighing less than four pounds each and had to stay in the neonatal intensive care unit for two months. With good diet and proper rest and exercise, I think we can get these twins to a healthy weight before they are born. At least, that's my hope.

39

Since the planet only takes 322 of its days to orbit the sun, I create a calendar of ten months, each of them thirty-two days except for the first two which are thirty-three days long. The Earth calendar was, of course, split into twelve months to roughly emulate the moon cycles. The word "month" is derived from moon. But on a planet with three moons, that twelve-month division is now unnecessary. I still think we need some kind of division of the year rather than just day numbers one through three hundred twenty-two. I keep the name of the months the same as our English months, just dropping January and February. I never liked those months anyway. And it makes sense to me that September would now be the seventh month, October the eighth, etc. The day we landed here therefore became March first of year one. Because the days are forty-six minutes shorter than days on Earth, a normal human pregnancy is now roughly forty-one weeks from the start of the last monthly cycle before conception rather than the forty weeks on Earth. That's assuming, of course, that we keep to a seven days per week calendar, and I see no reason to change that. Of course, I have to account for the the fact that I had Alexis change the duration of one second to make our days now register as twenty-four hours, even if they're not strictly twenty-four Earth hours. Changing the duration of the units of time doesn't change the processes of the human body though.

Lin gives birth to twin girls on November 10th of year 1. Both of them weigh just a little over five pounds. I would have liked to have seen them gestate a bit longer, but their small size seems to make the birthing process easier on Lin. Hal, of course, cries for most of the day, hating seeing his mother in any kind of pain. I try to soothe him as well as I can, but I am busy with Lin. Poor little guy has to sit in his bouncer and cry to himself most of the labor. Thankfully, he does sleep during the delivery. When he wakes up, he's suddenly a big brother. I pick him up and show him the two babies swaddled and sleeping in the bassinets from Transport One and Transport Two. Lin is exhausted, so I feed Hal a bottle of pumped breast milk and coax him back to sleep.

Later, I help Lin stand up and look down upon the sleeping girls.

"They're so little," she says. "I don't remember Hal being that small."

"He wasn't. He was almost eight pounds. These two are five-three and five-one."

We stand in silence looking at them for what seems like an hour but was probably only five minutes. I help her back to one of the other beds. I'll clean up the sheets of the birthing bed, made from the transport ship parachutes, later.

"You know," I say, "we probably conceived them in zero gravity. I wonder if that has anything to do with them being twins."

"I wish we could go back up there and do it in zero gravity again," Lin says. "See if we make another set of twins."

"That was pretty fun. I never realized how good we had it up there. It's been a constant struggle since we got here. Work, work, work. But I kept remembering how it felt to be outside under an open sky and not cooped up in a tin can. For what it's worth, I'm sorry I rushed us down here."

Lin smiles at me. "I'm sorry I've been so grumpy since we got here."

I shrug. "We can't change anything now. What we can do is figure out what to call these girls."

We have talked about naming them Stacey and Lilly after two of our missing crew members. Of course, Lin doesn't remember either of them. She only knows them from watching the videos of our mission training. And it seems awkward to name them after just two of the missing crew members while leaving out Kacey.

"What do you think?" Lin asks.

Like with naming Hal, something enters my head, and I just spout it out. "How about Faith and Hope?"

Lin considers this for a few seconds and then says, "I like it. Faith and Hope. What are they from?"

Kacey's Bible sits on the table next to me. I pick it up and hold it where Lin can see it. "A Bible verse from one of the Corinthians. I don't remember where. It goes something like 'These three remain: faith, hope, and love, but the greatest of these is love.'"

"What made you think of that?"

"I have no idea. I saw the Bible sitting there, and it just came to me."

"Faith and Hope. OK."

She smiles and kisses me. Just as she closes her eyes to sleep, one of the twins starts to cry. I go to pick her up, and the other one cries. Lin sighs and sits up. I hand her the first baby, Faith, to feed and go to get Hope.

With the arrival of Faith and Hope, we settle into a routine. I tend the garden for vegetables and my traps for meat while also caring for the babies. There are three now, and Lin only has two hands and two breasts. Hal takes his first steps just a few days after the twins are born. He then seems to skip the walking stage entirely, going from crawling to running. As busy as we are and as hard as we work to make a life here, there is still a whole lot of laughter in our house. Hope's weight drops to under five pounds a couple of days after she's born, but it quickly bounces back up. Both girls are healthy and seem to thrive. Lin and I sleep in shifts, and she pumps her breasts as often as she can so that I can feed the babies to give her a chance to sleep more than a couple of hours at a time.

We run out of the disposable diapers before the twins hit two months old. There is a supply of cloth diapers that had been vacuum sealed and didn't disintegrate on the trip from Earth, and these are invaluable. We begin leaving the diaper off of Hal and start potty training him early. There are many accidents, but he eventually catches on to using the toilet. The whole experience reminds me of potty training an adult Lin on the *Armstrong* which was, thankfully, a much easier process than training Hal.

"I'm dealing with a lot of shit," I say to myself one day as I'm cleaning up one of Hal's accidents not long after doing a little maintenance work on our primitive sewer line.

"What?" Lin asks.

I shake my head. "Nothing. Just thinking out loud."

She is feeding one of the babies, Faith I think. I have trouble telling them apart, but she seems to know instinctively which is which. The other is in her bassinet and is starting to fuss. I wash my hands as Hal continues to sit on the commode where I put him. The cloth diaper that we use as a towel is missing from the rack, so I shake my hands dry and pick up the other baby girl.

"Hey there," I say in my soothing voice.

She quiets down as I envelop her in my arms and she feels the heat from the skin on my chest.

"How are you—"

"Hope," Lin prompts.

"I was right. You are Hope."

Hope's eyelids blink heavily as she eases back toward sleep. Hal grabs and hugs my leg, and I sit down.

"Da," Hal says and climbs into my lap. He looks at his sister in my arms, reaches out, and caresses her face.

"This is Hope," I tell him.

"Ho."

I try not to laugh, but I am not completely successful.

"Not Ho. Hope. Hope."

"Hoo."

 "Well, Hoo is better than Ho."

As I watch Hal gaze lovingly at Hope, I am reminded of our unusual family dynamic. There are no other humans here. Hope isn't just Hal's sister; she is a potential future wife. Everything in me screams that I have to prevent this from happening, that it's wrong. Siblings don't have sex with each other and don't marry each other. But here, if they don't, then the human race will die out, and we will have come out here for nothing. Hal loves Hope now like a big brother ought to love a little sister. How can I allow that to become anything else?

"Are you okay?" Lin asks me.

"Huh?" I look at Lin and relax my expression. "Yeah. I was just thinking about how good of a big brother Hal is going to be."

Lin looks at Hal as he makes faces at Hope. He leans down to try to kiss Hope's forehead but doesn't quite get there as I have to keep my arm in front of him to keep him from waking the baby.

"That's sweet," Lin says.

"Da!" Hal says, standing up on my thigh and kissing me on the cheek.

He starts to fall, but I catch him with my free hand and guide him to the floor.

"I love you too Hal," I say as he runs to his mother and Faith.

40

Our life looks more like one on the frontier of nineteenth century North America than one set in the far future on a distant planet. We farm and trap for food, and most of the work we do is devoted to our continued survival. After the twins get a little bigger, I spend about an hour each evening digging a trench. Once I have that trench long enough, I dig another deep hole and then move the sewer line pipes into that trench, covering the pipes. I fill in the old hole, burying several months' worth of foul-smelling filth.

The evening after finishing the new sewer line, I test fly the drone from the old landing probe after charging it in the house for several days. Hal is outside with me as I fly it around our homestead. He laughs and jumps up and down every time I fly it close to us, which, of course, makes me laugh. I don't have a screen on the remote I rigged up for it, so I'm flying blind. But Alexis records the video it took, and we all watch it later. Hal gets a kick out of watching himself laugh on the flybys, laughing at his own cackling.

I usually work the garden in the early morning hours as the sun rises. Hal always wants to help, and I let him on occasion. His "help" is more of a hindrance, but I enjoy playing with him and making him feel like he's helping me. As the weeks go by without sighting any of those flying blue creatures, my work in the garden continues later and later into each morning, although I still always have the belt with the holstered Glock whenever I'm outside. I keep expanding the size of the garden, but the grass that grows on the plain is persistent, and I have to keep pulling new growth from the area I've already tilled.

We have a year-round growing season, and I harvest each crop when it needs to be harvested. The cornstalks grow quickly, and once I've pulled all the ears of corn from them, I pull up the old stalks and store them in the space under our house. Hal likes to play in the dirt that is left behind whenever I pull those stalks. He will sit and expand the hole before eventually filling it back in with dirt. Of course, he seems to wear as much dirt as he puts into those holes.

This is now the third full harvest of corn we've had. I have all the stalks pulled out of the ground and in a pile. I pick up a bunch to take them to the edge of the house, where I will have to crouch down and duckwalk them far enough under.

"Come on, Hal," I say.

He also likes to follow me under the house where he can walk at his full height. I think he likes having me closer to his own level.

"If I can get enough ears dry enough, I'll introduce you to popcorn," I say to him as I duck under the edge of what used to be Transport Three.

I drop my load and turn to see Hal out in the garden.

"Hal!" I say. "Get over here!"

He looks up and starts running toward me. I crawl toward the edge just as the blue thing sweeps out of the sky and grabs Hal in its talons. Hal screams, and I scream. "NO!!!!"

I have the gun in my hand, but the thing has flown up, and I have to get out from under the house to get a shot at it. By the time I do, the thing has moved Hal from its talons and into its mouth. I start shooting at it, screaming. *No, no, no, please not Hal! This can't be happening!*

I get off three rounds before the Glock jams, but all three miss. The thing has already flown so far away, across the plain toward the mountains. Lin stands in the doorway screaming. She saw that thing put Hal in its mouth. I'm screaming and crying too as I turn just in time to see her collapse in the doorway.

"Do something!" Lin urges, her voice almost a scream.

"Like what? That thing's over a hundred miles away by now. It would take weeks to get there and weeks to get back. And for what? Hal's already gone."

It breaks my heart to say it, that that sweet little boy is gone, food for that terrible creature. We don't even have a body to bury. Lin breaks down in sobs, and I put my arms around her, pulling her to me.

"I'm sorry. We got complacent." I don't want to say it, but it's my fault. I just assumed he was next to me since he always loved walking under the house with me.

"*We* got complacent?"

"*I. I* got complacent, ok? I did. I got complacent."

The girls are sleeping in their bassinets. Lin and I both gaze at them, thinking of Hal. This can't ever happen again. It sure can't happen to Faith and Hope. It shouldn't have happened to Hal. Why can't this day have never happened? Just rewind back to this morning and do it all over.

I stand and walk to the freezer, open it, and take out a thigh of one of those small deer. I leave it in the sink to thaw and sit back down next to Lin.

"I'm not hungry," she says as she stares at the sink.

"It's not for dinner."

She turns her stare toward Hal's empty bed and sobs. I stand back up and go to get the AR-15. I grab a fully loaded magazine and slide it into place and head outside. I walk in the open field past the garden, my arms held out with the rifle in one hand.

"Come on, you mother fuckers!" I yell. "Here I am!"

I scan the blue sky above, but I see no movement.

"So you only want to pick on my kids, huh? You afraid of me?"

There is nothing but the cloudless blue sky. I walk back inside. Lin has stopped sobbing and has Hope at her breast. Faith is awake in her bassinet but quiet so far. I stand the rifle in a corner and pick her up.

"My nipples ache," Lin says.

I know what she means. They ache at the loss of Hal.

She misses feeding him. Rather than break down crying again, I concentrate on what I have, on the beautiful baby girl in my arms.

"I'm sorry," I whisper to her, not wanting Lin to hear. "You had the best big brother, but he's gone now." And then the tears do fall.

When Hope finishes, Lin and I trade babies. Hope, her belly full, quickly falls asleep in my arms. I sit in one of the old cockpit chairs, not wanting to lay her down. Lin sniffles occasionally as we sit in silence. There doesn't seem to be anything to say. I can't get the image of that creature stuffing Hal into its mouth out of my head. I have never felt such helplessness in my life. Lin keeps holding Faith even after she finishes feeding her. The silence is oppressive, but there's nothing to say to relieve it.

41

By the time the meat thaws enough for me to cut it into strips, night has fallen. I leave it in the sink overnight and lie in bed looking at the ceiling. Neither Lin nor I sleep much. It took most of the day of grieving for Hal to remember what she said, that *we* hadn't been complacent, *I* had. I can feel her anger at me through the sadness and the tears. She blames me for this, and there is nothing I can ever do to make up for it. But I blame myself too. Yes, there isn't anything I can ever do to make up for it, either to Lin or myself.

"We have to keep going," I say in the semi-darkness of our room.

"What?"

"We have to keep going. I know we feel like we want

to curl up and die because Hal is gone, but we can't. We've got Faith and Hope, and we've got to keep looking out for them and each other."

"I know."

"I blame myself, and I know you blame me too."

"It wasn't your fault," Lin says.

"Yes, it was. I should have been more vigilant."

"It was that thing. It wasn't you."

She reaches over and caresses me in the way that tells me that she wants sex. It takes me a while to respond, but when I do, we make desperate, passionate love as if we are trying to block everything else in the universe out.

In the pre-dawn twilight, Hal is still gone. Yesterday really happened. I had prayed to a God that I believed in three billion years ago and one million light years away from here to take yesterday back, make it like it never happened. But yesterday did happen, and today nothing could change it.

After cleaning and loading the Glock, I cut the meat in the sink into thin strips and hang them on a rack like I had done weeks ago when trying to make jerky. I toss the machete out into grassy area just by the base of the stairs. The point hits the ground and stays, with the handle pointed up. I strap on the belt with the newly cleaned and loaded Glock in its holster, sling the rifle over my shoulder, and carry the rack of meat strips outside. I set the rack in the same spot I had put it the first time and run back to the space under the house, the same spot where I had been when I had seen Hal taken.

I get the rifle in ready position and wait. The rack with

the drying meat just sits, the light of the rising sun gradually inching over it. I hear the thing's flapping wings before I see it. Over the house it flies, sweeping down toward the meat. I fire, the shot hitting it in the head, blowing part of it away. The creature crashes to the ground, the rack of drying meat falling underneath it. I spring out from under the house, rifle in one hand and grabbing the machete with the other. The creature is writhing on the ground, bleeding from the large hole in its head, its wings sweeping through the grass in a wide circle. I stomp on the wings, holding the machete above my head, and burying the blade in its skull, cracking it open and expanding the hole the bullet made.

I leave the machete embedded in the creature's head as I turn and scan the sky, pointing the rifle up. I don't see or hear any more of the creatures. Shouldering the rifle, I yank the machete out of the thing's skull. There's no time to butcher it. Besides, I couldn't stand seeing the remains of Hal if I cut it open and it happened to be the one that grabbed him. I grasp it by the talons and drag it across the plain to the hole I dug for our waste and throw it in. Sweating and breathing hard by the time I'm done, I hurry back to the rack of meat, set it back up, and get back into my hiding place.

I wait another forty-five minutes before another one of those things swoops down toward the meat rack. I shoot it from a seated position under the house, but by the time I get out and on my feet, another creature is barreling right toward me. I raise the rifle and fire just as it arrives. Its head explodes at such a close range, but the body crashes into the side of the house, its talons slicing my left arm high near the shoulder and then slumping to the ground.

"Fuck you!" I say to the thing, but I have to turn my attention to the rest of the area.

The first creature is struggling to get upright, flapping its wings, trying to turn around. I fire at it again, hitting it in the back right between the flapping wings. It goes down in a heap. The bullet hit where I think the thing's spine ought to be. I walk out into the open, my head on a swivel between the thing on the ground and the air above me, with the rifle pointed up. The next creature is almost on me before I see the movement. I fire and hear the creature's awful scream of pain. It tries to land on me, but I push it away with the barrel of the gun and shoot it again, this time in the head.

I hear the flapping of wings above, and I see a blue swirl of them all spiraling downward toward me. I fire one shot after another at any little movement. I don't know how many shots miss, but three more of the things hit the ground near me. The rifle clicks when I've emptied the magazine. I toss it away and pull the Glock out of the holster. I have seventeen rounds in it, and I curse myself for not bringing spare magazines. Firing only when I'm sure I see one of them, I down four more of the things before there's a quiet lull.

What the hell is attracting them? I ask myself before glancing at the blood gushing out of the wound on my left arm.

Okay, now I know how to get your attention.

I spot the machete, still sticking up out of the ground, and I work my way over to it. I see a creature's open mouth above me, pink and black amidst all the blue, and I fire straight into it. The creature screeches and crashes just three feet away. I put another round in its head and pivot the barrel back toward the sky again.

Needing more cover, I grab the machete in my hand and head back toward the house. I can use it, but I'd be either in a crouch or on my knees and not able to move as quickly. That shouldn't be a problem unless I run out of ammo. The machete handle, wet with my own blood, almost slips out of my hand. I grip it tighter, wincing at the pain shooting down my arm, and fire at another one of the creatures. It veers away, rising and then falling to the ground. I reach the edge of the house, and I bend down and try to run underneath it, but I scrape my back along the edge. Falling, I roll under, holding the machete out away from me so that I don't roll onto the blade. Setting the machete aside, I roll onto my belly where I have a good view of the area on this side of the house. The garden is at the corner to my right, and one of the dead things is in the shadow of the house right next to it.

A creature flies down, trying to fly under the house right at me, and I shoot it at almost point blank range right between its eyes. The top of its head and its wings crash into the side of the house, and it falls right in front of me, blocking my view. I roll to my left, the gash in my arm screaming at me as the ground pulls it open as I roll. Two more of the things land out by the fallen rack of drying meat, and they become easy pickings. I fire a total of three rounds to take both of them down, cringing at having to use a third, but I've lost count of how many I have left.

Everything is quiet then and remains so for several minutes. I eject the magazine and see that I only have two rounds left in it. There should be one in the chamber, so I only have three more shots. I count fourteen dead creatures here on the grassy plain. With the one I dragged to our sewer dump, I've killed fifteen of them in one day. Just as I'm about to crawl out from under the house and head back inside, another one flies under the house from the other side. I turn and fire twice at it. The thing crashes into the landing gear of Transport Three and falls still.

"You bastards are smart," I say.

I turn all around, checking each side of the house, but I don't see any more. After crawling over to get the machete, I inch my way out from under the house, knowing I only have one more shot left.

"Alexis," I say, and I'm surprised by how hoarse my voice sounds. "Open the port hatch of Transport Two."

The stairs extend to the ground, and I dash up them, tripping on the last step and almost falling into the house. Lin is there to catch me, and she hits the button for the door to close immediately after I get inside. I am sweaty and bloody; I barely slept the night before; and my adrenaline rush is just about gone. Lin is saying something to me, but I'm not registering what it is. She takes my left arm and guides me toward the bed where I collapse.

42

When I awake, a bandage covers my left arm. Lin has washed the dirt and grime from my body. I peek under the bandage and see the stitches holding the gash together, and I begin to vaguely remember her suturing the wound. Gazing around our room, I'm struck by how little it resembles the transport space craft that it used to be.

One of the babies cries, and I hear Lin speak to her in a soothing tone. The room seems to spin when I sit up, so I stop moving after I swing my legs off the side of the bed. My headache is throbbing, and I consider just lying back down. I look to the window and see that it's almost dark outside. Or maybe it is night. It's difficult to tell if all three moons are up. The house feels so quiet without Hal running back and forth. My nose is stopped up, and I try sucking everything back in. That's when I get a whiff of something rotten.

"What's that smell?" I ask.

"What?"

Lin walks in the room with a baby in each arm.

"I said what's that smell?"

"I don't know."

"How long have I been out?"

"All night and all day."

"So you're telling me it's tomorrow night?"

"How are you feeling?"

I sigh. "I don't know. Woozy, I guess."

I stand on shaky legs and stagger into what passes as our main living area. Lin walks with me for support, but she can't even offer a hand while she carries the twins. I sit in my regular chair and hold my hands out for one of the babies.

"Are you sure? How's your arm?"

"It's fine. It hurts less than my head right now."

"Okay." Lin leans down to one side, and I take the baby.

"Hope?" I ask, looking at Lin.

"That's Faith."

"Oh." I am disappointed that I got it wrong, but I haven't gotten a really good look at her yet. I hold her out and look at her. "Hey Faith, how are you?"

I smile at her and am rewarded with a smile from the baby. I laugh, thinking that there's nothing better than seeing your baby smile at you. Hal used to smile at me all the time. The thought brings tears to my eyes, and one rolls down my cheek. No matter what I do and no matter how many of those creatures I kill, Hal will always be gone.

"Have you looked outside today?" I ask Lin.

She nods.

"Did you see any more of those creatures?"

She shakes her head. "Just the dead ones."

I nod while still making faces at Faith. "Good. I'll have to get out there and clear the dead ones. There's one right underneath the house."

"You should rest."

"I will. But I need to move them soon. That smell is only going to get worse."

We sit and entertain the babies for a few minutes. I try to make Faith laugh, but all I get are her sweet smiles.

"Are you hungry?" Lin asks.

"Starving."

She sets Hope in a bouncer and gets me a plate of venison and corn, taking Faith after she sets the plate in my lap.

I feel much better after I eat. Figuring that I won't be going back to sleep any time soon and that the smell emanating from under the house will only get worse, I reload my guns and head outside. I begin with the one under the Transport Three section of the house. My back still hurts from where I scraped it during the battle. That's how I think of it now, the battle. The smell of the thing is almost overwhelming. I hold my breath as I pull it out, and I have to take breaks to crawl out and get a breath of relatively fresh air. The other dead things are rotting too, so there is a general foul smell covering the area like a dark cloud.

The work of dragging all fourteen of the carcasses to the sewer pit takes all night. Only two of the moons are out, but they are both full or close to it, so there is plenty of light to see by. When I'm done, I gaze from the edge of the pit, thankful that the breeze is blowing the smell away from me and the house, and gaze at our home, a pentagon shaped structure in the middle of a grassy plain. It is a house of sadness and joy, sadness at the loss of Hal, joy at what we still have, Faith and Hope. I think of the American frontier, how settlers endured in spite of high mortality rates from enemy attacks, disease, and primitive health care.

I am dirty and sweaty again, and my bandage is hanging on my arm by a single strip of tape. Blood seeps through the stitches which have been stretched but have held together. Yet, I am hesitant to go inside. The place will still feel so empty without Hal. The sun is rising in the east, so I stand and watch it. The reflecting off the clouds turns them purple, then red, then orange. It's beautiful. I wish Hal could see it. I wish Lin were out here at my side to see it.

I scan the sky, looking for any of those flying monsters. I should be able to spot them since the color of the cloud cover is so different from their skin. But the skies are clear. There was some intelligence, especially with the one who tried to attack me from the other side of the house. Hopefully, some of them witnessed the battle and communicated with others. If they are the apex predators of this planet or even of the continent, they've probably never felt fear. Hopefully, I've instilled it into them with yesterday's battle. And just maybe, they have learned to avoid this area. Because this area has a new apex predator. At least, until our ammo runs out.

43

There are thirty-one of us now. We've lost seven, two to illness, three during childbirth, one to a horrible accident, and one, Hal, to one of those flying monsters. Lin was one of the ones lost during childbirth. It was during Maybelle's birth, our thirteenth child, in July of year 16. I was able to save the baby, but Lin hemorrhaged after a placental abruption and just lost too much blood. I held her hand during her final moments. She looked at me, her face a pale white, her body trembling, and said, "I'll wait for you, but take your time."

I took her loss hard. She was my companion, my rock, my best friend, and my lover. And she was the mother of all humanity. This certainly isn't the happy ending I would have written for myself. Of course, if I had been writing my own ending, I would have created a portal through time and space and gone back to twenty-first century Earth. I would have shown Lin where I grew up, where I lived in South Dakota, and the wonders of the big cities in the United States. I would have taken all our children and grandchildren with us, shown them all the things that the human race could achieve over time.

But this is our reality, and portals through time and space are not part of it. And there are no endings, happy or otherwise. Life goes on. I am an old man now, with eleven living children and nineteen living grandchildren. Helen, my oldest grandchild, is pregnant with my first great grandchild. We are in year 48 on this planet which I stopped calling Eden after losing Hal. It is not anything close to a paradise. But it is, now, our home. I think I'll rename the planet Lin. It's as a good a name for a planet as any. And it is my favorite name in the universe.

I have not seen another of those flying blue creatures since the day of the battle. They have left us alone, altering their hunting and traveling patterns, I suppose. This has resulted in a lot more animal life on the plains. The animals that I call little deer now routinely graze out in the open. I've only ever killed as much as we can eat, but that has grown throughout the years as we add more mouths to feed. Those little deer aren't as prevalent on the plain as they used to be. But we have found other species, both in the forest and on the plain, some of which make even better eating than those deer.

Two of my sons made an expedition to the distant mountains to the south in the year 22. They were gone for five months and came back with stories of fantastic creatures, one of which sounded like a mythical unicorn from old Earth. Of course, they'd never heard of a unicorn, but their descriptions seemed to fit it. There's so much that we don't know about this planet, especially in the mountain regions where, Alexis figured, it was not practical to put one of the landing probes. My sons did have to dodge a few of the flying blue creatures, killing two of them, so I know the things are still around.

I have been celibate since losing Lin. In the interest of propagating the species, I've had to let go of many of the sexual morals I'd held on Earth, but I did establish a rule forbidding cross-generational coupling. My children can get together with each other but not with me or with any of the grandchildren. I figure, since I'd made that rule for them, I couldn't very well break it, especially with any of the daughters I had raised since birth. It still, even in this place with so few of us, doesn't seem right. There have been a lot more girls than boys born during our time here, almost as if nature knows we need more girls to build the population. All four of my surviving sons have had two wives. Again, I would have protested this in another life, but this is what needs to happen here.

There are four cabins on the plain within sight of our original house made of the three transport ships. My children built them mainly out of logs from the forest. They call them houses, but I can't help but think of them as log cabins. After having arrived here on the finest equipment twenty-first century America could produce, we now live a primitive life. The last view screen in the main house went out in the year 24, taking with it our ability to watch any of the videos in the library. The biggest loss of this was the video of Hal laughing as I test flew the old drone. We didn't spend time taking video or photos when we first got here. We didn't have phones or cameras other than those on the drones, so that video of Hal laughing during those flybys was the only recorded image of him we had.

Earth Kevin was forty-eight when he went through the training for this mission and had his memory uploaded. We are now in year 48 on this planet. Of course, we spent over a year before that fully awake on the *Armstrong* and eighteen years in stasis as our bodies grew to adulthood. Yes, the years are shorter now, but my body is far older than it was when my memories of Earth end. After all this time, those memories of Earth now seem different, like an old movie on DVD rather than in 8K definition and full color. Maybe they're different because they were implanted, or maybe they're different because of all the time that has passed since I woke up in this body. It doesn't really matter. I rarely think of life on Earth anymore. I'm too busy living here.

Life, while busy, is good. Yes, I miss Lin and all those we've lost. But I have a wonderful family here. We all work together for the greater good. I wish people on Earth would have realized this. We are all related here, the thirty-one of us, but we were all related on Earth too. There were just nine billion more of us then.

The human species here on Lin is still hanging by a thread, even after forty-eight years. There are only thirty-one of us, and we all live in the same small area. We could all be taken out by a random virus or a natural disaster at any time. I'm thinking that we need at least ten more generations before we can really branch out and ensure our survival. Until then, the struggle will continue.

I read Kacey's Bible daily. It's a connection to old

Earth, but more importantly, it is a connection to something greater than all of us. I still believe in a Creator. How could I not after seeing as much of this creation as I have? As vast as this universe is, I know that the Creator is even larger and more powerful than I could have ever imagined while on Earth. I will leave this Bible to my children after I'm gone. What happens to it after that is out of my control. What will future generations think of the stories and the wisdom contained in it? For that matter, will future generations know that their ancestors came from a planet far away, and that this holy book came with them? What will they make of the place names: Jerusalem, Egypt, Babylon, Rome, and others? They will have no points of reference, unless someone names places here on this planet after those place names in the Bible. It will be a miracle if my family grows over the generations to populate this planet like Earth was populated, but somehow, I know that that miracle is possible with this almighty Creator. I'm sad that he never spoke to me as he spoke with Adam or Noah or Abraham in the early days of Earth. Many of the people Earth Kevin knew back on the old world would sneer at my faith, but I can't ignore the subtle signs of God that I see all around me.

I have taught my children and grandchildren about this faith, that God is all around us, that He guided us to this planet just as He created us on the old one. I know I don't have much longer left to live. Although I am not that old by Earth standards, the years of toil and struggle have caught up with me. I am confident in a life after this one. What will it be like? Will I just see Lin and Hal and the other five we've lost on this planet? Or will I also see

Earth Kevin, Cynthia, and the three kids he had on Earth? I'm not ashamed to say that I have no idea. But whatever I find on that other side, I have faith that it will be good, a just reward for a life of loss, struggle, and pain.

Propagation

Acknowledgements

I could not have written this novel without the love and support of my wife Jennifer and of the rest of the family. I'd also like to thank the members of the DFW Writers Workshop for offering their thoughts and insights during the early stages.

I came up with the idea of using cloning and memory transference as a way for humanity to travel to the stars using our current space flight technology many years ago, but I didn't know what to do with it for the longest time. I still believed that it could make a fascinating story, but I was afraid to tackle it until recently. When I started writing this, I didn't have much of a plan. I let Kev tell his own story.

I also realize that there are still a lot of unanswered questions. How advanced are those humanoids on the other continent? What was that silver triangle that Kev saw? Ultimately, I decided that Kev was just going to have to be OK with never knowing the answers.

Kev and Lin's story is finished, but there could still be more stories on the planet Lin. Will I write those stories? I don't know. There are still so many things I want to explore in my writing here on Earth. But if you want to read about Kev and Lin's great-great grandkids (and future generations after that) let me know.

Thank you for reading *Propagation* and my other four books. Please stay updated on future works on my website https://www.dhjonathan.com.